Karen McCombie

THE PAST, THE PRESENT AND THE LOUD, LOUD GIRL

WITHDRAWN

Welcome to the weird and wonderful world of Ally Love, age 13...

ALLY'S WORLD

■SCHOLASTIC

~~for Lorne sausage banana~~
~~for Lorne sausage Bonella~~
~~for Lauren Banana~~
for Lauren Bonella!

Scholastic Children's Books
An imprint of Scholastic Ltd
Euston House, 24 Eversholt Street
London, NW1 1DB, UK
Registered office: Westfield Road, Southam, Warwickshire, CV47 0RA
SCHOLASTIC and associated logos are trademarks and/or registered
trademarks of Scholastic Inc.

First published in the UK by Scholastic Ltd, 2001
This edition published in the UK by Scholastic Ltd, 2010

Text copyright © Karen McCombie, 2001
The right of Karen McCombie to be identified as the author of this
work has been asserted by her.

ISBN 978 1407 11761 4

Printed in the UK by CPI Bookmarque, Croydon, Surrey.
Papers used by Scholastic Children's Books are made from wood grown
in sustainable forests.

1 3 5 7 9 10 8 6 4 2

www.scholastic.co.uk/zone

Contents

PROLOGUE

Dear Mum,
I've decided to do something.

Don't panic: it's not like I'm about to pierce my lip, or enrol for the next Mars mission, or run away with the circus and juggle clowns or something. (Although you'd probably think all that was cool.)

It's just that, you know how I've been keeping a box with all our photos and school reports and stuff for you to see? Well, no you don't – which is the problem – but trust me, that's what I'm doing.

Well, anyway, apart from those bits and pieces, I've decided that I'm going to start writing down some of the things that happen to all of us; the things that matter, anyway. It's not going to be like a diary or anything – I don't exactly have the patience for that. (Though I did buy one a couple of Januarys ago; it was half-price in the stationery shop up on the Broadway. I started out OK, prattling on about *what* I'd done that day and *what* I was feeling and *what* we'd had for tea, but by January 10th

1

I was just doodling flowers on the page. And the entry for January 15th just said "BORED, BORED, BORED", so I kind of chucked it in after that.)

So this time, I think I'll do it like an essay… Only it might be a bit on the long side. You know what I'm like. Remember that last report you saw when I was at primary school? *"Ally is very bright and imaginative, but her mind does tend to wander…"* Hey, guess what? Nothing's changed. It's like Grandma says, I'd get twice as much done if I stopped wittering for five minutes. Which is sort of true, I know. And which is what I'm doing now, I suppose…

OK, so back to my plan.

I think I'll do it like I'm writing it for some stranger to read, 'cause – sorry, I don't mean to give you a hard time about this – it might make me too sad if I just set it all down for you. I suppose that's because I know it's not exactly likely that you're going to come walking through the door in the next two minutes or anything, and beg to read this…

But then, if – by some mind-blowing magic – you did, you'd have all our pictures and things to look at, *and* be able to read all my stories about what's been going on with me and Linn and Rowan and Tor. And, of course, Dad.

Speaking of Dad, I think I'll start with his fortieth

birthday, 'cause that was when Kyra turned up, and when – don't panic – we nearly lost Tor…

Love you lots,
Ally
(your Love Child No. 3)

Chapter 1

WELCOME TO MY (WEIRD) WORLD...

Look at a map of the world, and find Britain (small, jaggedy, sort of in the middle).

Look at a map of Britain and find London (big blob, down in the south).

Look at a map of London and find Crouch End (weird name, nice place).

Look for Palace Heights Road (number 28, to be precise).

When you find number 28, stand on the pavement opposite and look at the terraced house with your eyes half-crossed (all fuzzy like that, it seems almost as posh as the ones on either side of it. *Un*cross your eyes and you'll see that it's actually pretty tatty round the edges).

I'm Ally Love, and this is where I live with my dad (Martin), a power-mad control freak (my seventeen-year-old sister, Linn), a complete airhead (my fifteen-year-old sister, Rowan) and a space cadet (my seven-year-old brother, Tor).

OK, so now look up, past the big bay living-room

window, past the first-floor bay (my sister Rowan's room) until you see a tiny window at the top – my attic bedroom.

That's where I've woken up nearly every morning for all of the thirteen years I've been on this planet, and where I'm normally very happy to wake up. Except for one particular morning...

It was weird – for some reason, my whole head was vibrating.

But then, there are plenty of weird things in this world. Like nose hair. I mean, if the point is that it's there for protection, then why doesn't it grow in your mouth too? (Blee...)

And electricity. It doesn't matter how many times the principle's explained to me, I still don't get it. But don't get me wrong, I am pretty *pleased* about it. Dad sometimes likes to light these big, fat, coloured candles we have in the living room, but until they invent a candle-powered TV (that would need a *really* big, fat candle, I guess), I'm OK with electricity, however weird it is.

Of course, plenty of people – including my oldest sister – think our parents are weird for giving their kids odd names (me, I got off lightly out of the four of us), but I think it just goes to show that some people have no imagination. And anyway, when they get to know the story behind each name, they usually think it's pretty cool after all.

Oops, there I go. Getting sidetracked by weird stuff when I was supposed to be talking about the head-vibrating thing. But I do that a lot (get sidetracked, not have a vibrating head) – so get used to it.

Anyhow, it was a Sunday morning when I felt my head vibrate. At first I didn't panic; I just told myself that there must be a giant articulated lorry parked in the street outside, its engine throbbing so hard that it was shaking the house from the foundations right up to my little room under the eaves. That, or maybe it was a low-flying plane, rumbling through the skies above our house, sending tremors from the roof tiles down.

Then I noticed something else – one side of my face and neck were as hot as a very hot thing. A vibrating head *and* a burning-hot face...

OK, so *then* I started to panic. Compared to people like my airhead sister Rowan and my ditzy best mate Sandie, I know I come over like I'm confident and logical. But underneath, I'm basically a world-class worrier...

What had they told us at school about meningitis? Did the telltale signs include victims hearing a persistent droning noise that made their heads vibrate? Was it a common sign to feel one side of your face burning up? I couldn't remember.

Then all of a sudden, the noise and the vibration stopped. In its place, there was silence, broken only by one small noise.

"Snurph."

My eyes flicked open. I was awake, and instantly flooded with relief.

I didn't have the first warning signs of meningitis.

I wasn't about to be carted off to the Whittington hospital down the road.

I turned my head on the pillow and found myself nose to nose with Colin.

"Don't mind me," I muttered, as he moved in his sleep, settling himself more comfortably in the cosy pile of people fur that he'd come across.

As I tried to pull my long, brown hair slowly out from under him, he gave another snuffly cat snore and started off with his loud, droning purr again.

Freeing myself, I flung back the duvet and left Colin to it. I padded over the old, worn carpet and did the morning ritual I've done ever since I was tall enough to reach the ledge on my tiptoes – staring out of my tiny window at the view of the Palace, perched on top of one of London's only proper hills.

"Well, Ally Love," I said to myself, "You could

7

have been famous; you could have gone down in medical history as the first person to suffer from Vibrating Head Syndrome."

I shot a glance backwards in the direction of Colin, who was now sprawling his whole body and three legs (hey, I'll explain later) across the whole pillow.

Then I thought of something *truly* weird: do cats' heads vibrate when they purr?

I walked back over to Colin, and clamped my fingers round his face.

"Yeee-oow!"

My scientific experiment didn't prove the vibrating theory. What it did do was show that cats really, *really* don't appreciate having their heads squeezed when they're sleeping.

Trust me, I've got the bite-marks to prove it.

Now that I knew I wasn't going to die (well, eventually, yeah – but not right that *second*), I should have been skipping down the stairs to breakfast with a stupid grin of relief on my face.

But I didn't. Mainly because my fear of immediate death had been replaced by an ominous feeling that I'd forgotten something...

Uh-oh.

Chapter 2

LINN'S LOUSY IDEA

"What's up with your hair? You look like you've been dragged through a forest backwards," said my big sister Linn, staring up at me and wrinkling her nose.

"A cat slept on my head."

"Oh," shrugged Linn, carrying on buttering her toast. "Which one?"

"Colin," piped up my little brother, as I sat down at the kitchen table beside him.

"How did you know that?" I asked, rubbing at my nose where it was tickly with stray cat-hairs.

"Ginger fur stuck on your face," Tor muttered, reaching over and pointing his finger right into my cheek.

"Oh."

"And that – that's Colin's teeth-marks."

"Thank you, Pet Detective," I mumbled, looking down the hand that Colin's fangs had dented.

Here's the thing: I close my door every night before I go to bed, but always in the morning some animal's worked magic and wangled its way in (but usually into some cosy corner – getting comfy on my head doesn't happen too often). And I include my little brother Tor in that. It's pretty sweet, actually – whenever Tor has nightmares, which isn't often – it isn't my dad, or Rowan, or Linn he scampers to. It's *my* bed he ends up curling up at the bottom of, like one of the army of hamsters and gerbils he's got stashed in cages all around his own room.

"Rowan up yet?" I asked, helping myself to orange juice from the sticky carton in the middle of the table.

I still hadn't figured out what the thing was that I'd forgotten. Maybe when I was more awake it would come to me...

"You're joking, aren't you? Haven't you noticed it's only half-nine?" mumbled Linn with her mouth full. "The Queen of the Night won't be gracing us with her presence for ages yet."

That was true – Rowan never got up much before noon at the weekends, much to our grandma's disapproval, *and* Linn's. But then Linn gets snippy and grouchy at Rowan pretty easily.

Honestly, my two sisters are about as different as people can get and still be related. Linn is seventeen and sensible, and likes everything neat, tidy, organized and lined up with a set square (believe me, she *would* if we let her). Which is a bit of a shame for Linn, since she has to live in a wonky, ramshackle house like ours. And our whole family's pretty ramshackle and wonky too, when you think about it, and that doesn't please Linn too much either.

You should see her room – it's on the other side of the attic from mine. Where mine's painted sky blue (kind of fitting for an attic, don't you think? The room closest to the real thing?), with posters and pictures and my big old map of the world covering most of the wall space, Linn's is the exact opposite. Everything's so white and streamlined and minimal you'd think she'd ironed it all, from the carpet to her textbooks. Sometimes I catch Linn in there, sitting on the window seat and staring out at her view of central London sprawling away in the distance (approximately eleven and a quarter kilometres, fact fans). At times like that, locked away in her little oasis of calm and non-clutter, I get the feeling that the one thing she'd love to do is get away from sleepy Crouch End – and us.

Now take Rowan's room. You think our living room's bad, with those canary-yellow walls and the navy woodwork? (Mum's choice, by the way, like every other colour scheme in the house except our own bedrooms). Well, Rowan's room is something else. At the moment she's painted it raspberry, and it's like an explosion in a fairy-lights factory. She's got them draped everywhere: round the bay window, along the shelves, the wooden bedhead, and, once, even round Tor.

Rowan had just taken a photo of him all decked out in blinking lights, when Linn barged in and yanked them off him, accusing Rowan of trying to electrocute our little brother. Of course, she was totally right, in a strictly speaking, safety-conscious way, but sometimes I think that Linn doesn't know how to have fun. After all, Tor *did* look pretty cute (and bemused) in the photo, and he didn't seem to mind too much. But then Tor never grumbles about anything. Mainly 'cause he never says much, ever.

If Rowan could get away with wearing fairy lights, I think she'd do it. She's fifteen now, but ever since I can remember, show her anything that twinkles and glistens and she's completely sold on it. It's like with her clothes – ages ago, she bought all these little-old-lady beaded cardies for about zero pence from jumble sales and second-hand shops and wore them all the time. She got loads of weird looks and sniggery comments for it, and then BLAM! everyone from Miss Selfridge to New Look starts selling them.

And you should see the piles of fashion magazines she's got in her room. One stack of *Elle*s comes up to my waist practically, and they've been sitting there so long she's stuck this mad old tasselly table lamp on top.

So, my two older sisters have got different tastes, but that isn't the main reason Linn gets bugged by Rowan. The main reason is that Rowan insists on doing the one thing that no one else does – she calls Linn by her full name: Linnhe.

Boy, does Linn hate that name. I remember her blowing up at my dad once, saying it was cruel of parents to give their kids weird names. I can't remember how Dad reacted – he probably just nodded and agreed with her. It's his usual way of avoiding arguments. But I'm with Rowan on this – not that I'd dream of saying so to Linn. I think Linnhe (think: Linny) is really pretty. Still, Linn hates it so much that she changed it to the more normal sounding Linn. She even went so far as to try and change the spelling to Lynne, but it got too complicated; her name was spelt the old way on everything from her school records to the "Property of Linn Love" notes that she sticks on everything she owns. Including her favourite yoghurts in the fridge. Honest – I'm not joking.

"So, where's Dad?" I asked Linn, sloppily

spreading some peanut butter on my toast.

"Out getting a newspaper," said Linn. "And listen, speaking of Dad, I'm a bit worried…"

I paused – was my forgotten thing something to do with Dad? Nah – that didn't feel right. I carried on with my peanut butter.

"Worried? How come?" I asked her, through a mouthful of toast.

"Well, we have a problem…" she sighed.

"Houston, we have a problem…" muttered Tor in a fake American accent.

He watched a programme about rocket launches the night before with Dad, if you want an explanation. But then Tor and his little ways don't need explaining, if you just grasp the single fact that he's a bit of a space cadet in general.

For example, at that moment, I noticed he was drawing a smiley face with his finger in the margarine on his toast, which was completely normal. For *him*, I mean, not necessarily for *every* seven year old. But *our* seven-year-old brother has the habit of moulding *all* his food into some kind of artwork before he eats it. He's very good with scrambled eggs – makes them look like clouds in the sky on his plate. That's why he hates soup; it's really hard to do anything artistic with a bowl of mushroom soup. Try it if you don't believe me.

"What kind of a problem?" I asked my sister dubiously.

The reason I felt a bit dubious is that Linn sees practically *everything* as a problem. Tor merrily announcing that he's found a new walking-wounded, stray animal to clutter up the house with is a major problem. Me leaving my homework till Sunday night is worthy of a drama. Rowan sitting daydreaming instead of taking her turn doing the dishes is virtually an arrestable offence.

Linn gazed at me in despair; I was obviously meant to *know* something, or be *aware* of something. Oops. Since I hadn't a clue what that might be, I just gazed back at her, wondering how she always managed to look so unnaturally together first thing in the morning. It wasn't fair. Her blonde-ish fair hair was dragged neatly back into a ponytail, and unlike me and Tor – who were still in our pyjamas (me: baggy, drawstring-waist trousers and an old T-shirt; Tor: a Wallace & Gromit number) – Linn was already dressed in her regulation black trousers (she has about seventeen thousand pairs, I swear she does) and zip-necked top.

My eyes dropped – as they often do – to the outline of her perfectly formed boobs in that tight top. I was thinking – as I often do – how was it that fate gave her a proper-sized chest, as *well* as everything else, when all *I* got from the Love family gene pool was two mini-mounds that have trouble filling a double-A bra? ("Plenty of time for them to grow!" Grandma always trots out whenever I moan about it. Well, I'll try to be patient – but I won't hold my breath...)

"Don't you realize the date?" Linn said wearily, making me flip my gaze back up to her face smartish. "It's Dad's birthday two weeks tomorrow – and it's his fortieth. What on earth are we going to get him?"

"Uh ... a present?" I ventured, knowing I was probably saying the wrong thing.

Tor must have thought so too – he stopped what he was doing and eyed us both warily. Out of the corner of my eye I could see that he was obviously inspired by my encounter with Colin. Beside the smiley face he'd traced in the margarine, he'd been moulding a wobbly, vaguely cat-shaped dollop of gingery marmalade.

"Yes, I *know* we've got to get him a present," said Linn irritably – still, not as irritably as it could have been, knowing her. "But what *kind* of present? I mean, it's got to be special, since it's his fortieth. And it's up to us to make it special; after all, who else will?"

I knew what – or rather who – she was getting at: Mum, of course. But I wasn't in the mood to get into all that.

"Mmm, it *would* be nice to do something special..." I agreed non-committally.

Agreeing with Linn is always the easiest way to go. Like I said, even *Dad* knows that.

"Well," she said, suddenly losing the anxious look, and seeming quite chuffed with herself. "I've had an idea."

"Oh, yeah?"

Me (doing the talking) and Tor (just listening) were both on tenterhooks waiting for this. Whatever was coming wasn't just an idea that we could all kick about and discuss. Whatever Linn had thought of was probably going to happen.

"I thought," she began, a conspiratorial grin breaking out on her face, "that we should ... have a surprise party for him!"

Right away, I knew I needed to set her straight, remind her that sweet, shy people like our dad don't really respond to the whole "Oh my goodness – all this for little old *me*?!" centre-of-attention thing. And I needed to remind her that after four years of looking after us on his own (with a little help from Grandma, of course), he hadn't exactly got a lot of time for keeping up friendships. The surprise was, who exactly was she planning to *invite* to this surprise party?

But of course, I am speaking about my sister Linn – She Who Must Be Obeyed – here.

"Yeah! That sounds like a great idea!" I lied through gritted teeth.

Chapter 3

SENSIBLE ANSWERS ONLY, PLEASE

Considering that my friends' houses are all magnolia-painted neat, with matching towels and plate sets – and chairs, for that matter – it's quite reassuring to know that there's another building in the area that's as beautiful, but as crumbly round the edges as my house.

I ended up thinking just that, sitting on a bench in the park surrounding Alexandra Palace and gazing up at the huge Rose window of the Palace itself. I'd come to the park with the dogs after my conversation with Linn about Dad's birthday present. Walking clears my head, and right now, I knew I needed to come up with an alternative plan to Linn's – and quick.

But so far, of course, all I'd done was daydream.

See, Alexandra Palace is this stunning, big building from a distance, but up close, OK it's *still* amazing, but it's sort of tatty round the edges. One side of the building's semi-restored and shiny, and the other is semi-smoke-damaged and boarded up. It's really sad when you imagine how awesome it would have looked (all sandstone and glass domes) when it was first built back in 1800-whenever. But then not a lot of people ever had a chance to see it that way – the whole place caught on fire sixteen days after it was finished. What a bummer.

Not that I'm saying a fire or anything that drastic has ever happened to *our* house. It's just that, while it's a really comfy, pretty place to live in, there's loads wrong with it. It's the kind of house where there's always handles falling off the kitchen cupboards and window frames with big, breezy gaps in them and pipes in the wall that sometimes gurgle like they're about to throw up. That's not even *starting* on stuff like the sofa my dad brought home after he "salvaged" it from a skip (it was so full of fleas that the *cats* refused to sit on it), or the ominous cracks in loads of the walls and ceilings that keep getting bigger and bigger ("Subsidence," my grandma occasionally points out darkly). But I wouldn't swap our house – even though it does look like a cross between a craft fair and a second-hand shop – in a million years. (Linn, of course, *would* – in a *micro*-second.)

So, it was late morning on Sunday, and I was sitting staring at the stained glass of the Rose window, views of distant high-rises in central

London behind me, when this frenetic barking started up.

Rolf (our big, hairy dog) barks at anything – the postman, the gate-post, traffic cones, blades of grass, you name it – but the fact that Winslet (our small, hairy dog) was barking too meant only one thing: Billy and Precious were on their way.

I was glad – I wanted to sound out Billy, since he was a boy, about any ideas he had for a good present for *my* dad. OK, so Billy is my age and twenty-seven years *younger* than my dad, but they're both males, so I figured he might come up with *something* useful. I knew I was clutching at straws, but I was desperate to go back home with at least *one* alternative suggestion to Linn's rotten surprise-party idea.

"Hi!" I waved at him, as he stomped over the grass towards me.

"Hi, Ally!" Billy grinned, flopping down beside me on the bench.

Billy's my mate; we've known each other since we were – ooh! – *that* high. I sometimes don't see him too often during the week since he goes to a different school from me (Muswell School for Boys), so whatever we're doing, we always try to meet in the park on Sunday mornings to catch up. He comes over from his side of the Palace

(Muswell Hill), I wander over from mine (Crouch End), and we meet in the middle, on the grass just downhill from the Rose window.

"So how's it going?" Billy asked, keeping one eye on the typical mayhem going on in front of us.

All three dogs were tearing round in a big blurry bundle, playing their favourite game, which involves lots of running in circles, barking and occasional growling (Winslet). Translated into people speak, the game is called "Aw, Go On – Let Me Smell Your Bum!", and the object of it is for Billy's small, white, irritating poodle to attempt to sniff the bottoms of *my* dogs, while Rolf and Winslet do everything short of biting Precious to get him to stop. Personally, I think they're both too polite.

"I'm OK," I shrugged. "What about you?"

"Yeah, great," said Billy unconvincingly. "Except for the fact that I failed two tests at school this week, everyone gave me a hard time 'cause I let in three goals at five-a-side yesterday afternoon, and that really pretty new girl that's just moved in on my street still doesn't know I exist."

At the mention of school, I immediately felt that faint, worrying flutter at the back of my mind again. What *was* it I'd forgotten? I waited for a second, giving my brain a chance to explain itself, but when nothing happened, I turned my attention back to Billy.

"But you said that girl looks about eighteen," I pointed out, knowing I was about to burst his bubble. "She's not exactly going to be tripping over herself to talk to you, is she?"

I'd been starting to notice that Billy was getting a bit predictable lately. We used to have these great conversations about life, PlayStations and everything, but nowadays, he'd always work the conversation round to girls, sooner or later. He was desperate for a girlfriend (that much was obvious), and kept asking me for advice about how you get together with someone and what you do once you *are* together. Like I was some big expert or something. I've only ever been out with one boy – Keith Brownlow – and that only lasted a few dates. (What a disaster my love life is – just don't get me started, OK? I know eight year olds who've had more snogs from boys than me...) Anyway, if you must know about Keith Brownlow, well, *I* decided to chuck *him* when he kissed me right after he'd finished a can of Coke.

(Hot tip, boys: belching in a girl's mouth is *not* too gorgeous.)

"Just kick me now, why don't you," mumbled Billy, pretending to be hurt at my home truths about his chances with the hot-chick neighbour.

"Don't tempt me," I said, aiming a trainer in his

23

direction. "Anyway, there's something I need your help with. It's my dad's fortieth birthday soon. What do you reckon we should get him?"

"A Zimmer frame? Grey hair-dye? Ouch!"

I didn't kick him hard, really I didn't. But boys are such drama queens, aren't they?

"Billy! Stop mucking about and help me out!" I nagged him.

"*I* don't know what you should get him, do I?" Billy mumbled, rubbing his shin. "I mean, he's *your* dad. *You* should know what he wants."

"Well, if I did, I wouldn't need to ask *you*, would I?"

It was my own fault. I should have known it was a waste of time bringing up the subject with him. Billy can quote huge chunks of dialogue out of movies and could tell you the name of every weird alien in every series of *Star Trek*, but he's pathetically hopeless at anything remotely normal and useful.

"What about your sisters?" he asked me. "Doesn't Linn have everything organized? She usually does…"

Billy's pretty intimidated by Linn, and you can't really blame him for that – I think she'd be capable of intimidating the Prime Minister if she was in the right mood (make that *wrong* mood). Whenever Billy comes round to my house for tea he goes really quiet in front of her. But then, he's kind of funny about Rowan and Tor too. He thinks they're weird; Rowan 'cause of the way she dresses and everything, and Tor (Billy calls him "Spook Kid") because he just sits and stares silently over the table at Billy, which is what he tends to do with *any* of the friends we bring home. (Tor even does it to his *own* little buddies, but I guess they mustn't mind, 'cause they still want to hang out with him.)

"You don't want to hear what *Linn*'s thought of. C'mon, Billy – what would be your dream present?"

"Dunno, really," he replied, frowning. "But this morning, I was thinking how cool it would be to own a life-sized cardboard cut-out of Lara Croft."

"Billy, a life-sized cut-out of Lara Croft would be about ten centimetres high. Get it through your head – she's not real. You're in lust with a very small character in a computer game. No wonder you can't get a proper girlfriend!"

I could see that he was struggling with a smart comeback line, but bless him, Billy's not really great at sparkling wit. I mean, he's got a great sense of humour and everything, but he's no match for me. Which is fun. For me.

Not that I can talk, of course, considering the only boyfriend I've got right now is Billy – and that's "boy" and "friend" with a very *big* space between both words…

"Oh, yeah? Yeah?" he fumbled around, hoping vainly that something smart and cutting would come to him. "Well Lara Croft *isn't* just a computer character. What about the *Tomb Raider* movie? She's in that!"

"The thing about the *Tomb Raider* movie," I sighed, "is that it's a *movie*. It's not real life – and just 'cause some actress is playing Lara Croft doesn't make her real either!"

"I know that!" said Billy defensively.

It was a stupid conversation, but then it's pretty typical of the stupid conversations we have. Sometimes Billy drives me crazy when we end up yakking round in circles like this, but most of the time it's kind of fun, actually.

I was just about to tell him that even if Lara Croft suddenly did come to life, he had a better chance of going with one of the Teletubbies than her, when we got disturbed by a sudden kerfuffle.

"Precious!" Billy yelped. "Oi! Precious! C'mere! Oh, God – he's off. Hold on, Al, I'd better go and grab him."

I watched as Billy hurtled down the hill to where the pint-sized poodle was trying to do slightly *more* than sniff the bums of two puzzled Dalmatians. The guy who owns those Dalmatians isn't exactly the world's biggest smiler at the best of times. A small yappy dog trying to ram its nose up the bottoms of his prize pooches was definitely *not* going to bring a warm, sloppy grin to his face.

And poor Billy – no wonder he let three goals in and couldn't get a girlfriend. Just watching him run, watching the way his long, skinny legs and arms loped about all over the place, you could tell that he was a complete stranger to the art of coordination. That's the thing: Billy is *almost* what you could call good-looking, but he's such a clumsy geek that no girl in the Western Hemisphere is ever going to mistake him for Brad Pitt in a hurry.

"Precious! Come here! Precious – heel! Now!" I heard him yell to a totally oblivious dog.

Precious. Can you *believe* that Billy's mum came up with that name for their dog, knowing that her poor son was going to have to use it every time he took the thing for a walk? I'm sure there must be a clause in the Children's Act somewhere that says it's cruel to make thirteen-year-old boys shout "Precious!" loudly in a public place. What was the woman thinking of?

I mean, shouting "Rolf" and "Winslet" gets you the odd look from people in the park – people whose own dogs must be called Dullsville stuff like "Spot" or "Rover" or something – but it's a thousand times better than "Precious". Who is, in fact, about as precious as a flu virus.

Both my dogs suit their names, I reckon. Rolf – a pedigree mongrel from a long, distinguished line of mongrels – was our first ever pet; Dad got him from Wood Green Animal Shelter as a distraction for Tor when our little brother suddenly clocked that our mum wasn't around any more. Since it was his dog, Tor was allowed to name him. And since his favourite programme in the world used to be something called *Animal Hospital*, presented by a beardy bloke called Rolf Harris, Rolf it was.

We ended up with Winslet a couple of years ago when Rowan and Tor found her wandering about in the park, dishevelled, hungry and grumpy (her natural state, we found out later). They did the right thing and took her along to the police station, where Dad inevitably ended up ticking the box on the details form saying we'd take her if she wasn't claimed. She wasn't. So, since Tor already had built up quite a little menagerie at our place by this time, all of whom he'd named, the honours went to him again. He'd just seen *Titanic* and had a huge crush on Kate Winslet, so Winslet she became. (Actually, it was Kate at first, but somehow "Kate" didn't really suit a small, hairy, grumpy dog too much.)

Billy came plodding back up the incline,

an indignant poodle writhing in his arms, and breathlessly plonked himself back down next to me.

"You know, if you want to get your dad something special," he panted (Billy, not Precious), "then I think you should get him something original, something he'd *never* think of..."

"Yeah? Like what?"

I was intrigued. It sounded like Billy might just be a lot less useless than I'd thought.

"Huh?" he blinked at me, trying not to lose his grip as Precious wriggled around, trying to escape. "I dunno. That's as far as I got."

"Billy," I said wearily, "your *dog*'s smarter than you."

As if to show off how smart he was, Precious attempted to lunge enthusiastically towards me.

I jerked back, just out of licking range.

There was no *way* Precious was getting within half a metre of my face. Not knowing where that nose had been last...

Chapter 4

SANDIE AND HER AMAZING WRIGGLING HAIR...

All the way home, I racked and racked my brains for some amazing present idea, but I think I'd used up all my energy for the day. Me and Billy had walked the dogs till *they* were tired, *we* were tired, and every other dog-walker in a hundred-metre radius was tired of Precious lungeing his small self at their pets.

My eyes were glued to the pavement, like that might help my concentration or something, when a few doors down from our house, I heard Rowan. She'd got these new mules in a sale, and you could recognize the *flippety-flap, flippety-flap* of them three streets away.

"Rowan!" I called after her. My sister's mind works in mysterious ways – if anyone could come up with something unusual and special for Dad, Rowan could. "Where are you going?"

"Just up to the shop," she called back, holding up her hand to shield the sun from her eyes, the multi-coloured Indian bangles she wore jangling down her arm. "We're out of loo roll."

See, that's Rowan for you: who else goes to the corner shop for loo roll in red velvet mules?

"Uh, OK – I'll see you in a bit."

I'd catch her later, I decided, and pick her brain. Tor's too – just 'cause he was little didn't mean he couldn't come up with a smart idea.

Thinking so much about Dad, I jumped guiltily as I walked in the front door and came face-to-face with him.

"Hi, babe! Been walking the mutts, then?"

He's so laid-back and nice, my dad. I know people are meant to love their parents, but I sometimes think they don't seem to *like* them all that much. But with my dad, I think I'd like him even if I was just meeting him for the first time.

My best friend Sandie, she's kind of proof of that; she's round at our house *all* the time, and is always saying how cool my dad is. It's actually a bit of a joke in my house how often Sandie comes round. She does this thing where she seems to leave another bit of clothing or another CD every time she's here; Dad says he thinks she's trying to move in without anyone noticing.

"Hi, Ally!" said Sandie, appearing from the kitchen, a cup of coffee in her hand.

See what I mean?

"Listen, Ally Pally—"

That was my dad. He always calls me that.

"—I'm going along to the workshop for an hour. A whole load of spare parts came in yesterday, and I want to get them sorted out before I open up tomorrow."

"OK," I shrugged and smiled at him. It was perfect, really; if he was safely out of the house, I'd have the chance to talk to Rowan and Tor and even Sandie about ideas for a present without worrying that he'd overhear.

But hold on – the Ally Pally thing. Maybe you'll want to know what that's all about. And if I tell you that, I guess I might as well tell you about all our names while I'm at it. Basically, while my dad had a hand in them, they're all Mum's fault. Which I'm pretty glad about.

So, when it came to naming their Love children (as Mum and Dad liked to call us), it happened like this...

First up, there's Love Child No. 1: Linnhe. Mum and Dad were young, happy, but skint, and had borrowed my grandma's car to go on a camping holiday in Scotland. The plan was to see as many castles and lochs as possible, and the day they checked out Inverlochy Castle on Loch Linnhe was the day my mum sussed out that she was pregnant. When my sister was born, my folks were reminiscing about the trip to Scotland, and it just kind of seemed perfect to call her Linnhe. Linn might not agree, but I think she should count her blessings. The day before, they'd been camping beside Loch Fyne. With a name like Fyne Love, you could imagine the stick she'd get from lads at school. Mind you, it would have come in handy if she'd chosen a career in X-rated videos, I suppose.

Rowan, Love Child No. 2, was due to come along next, and by this time my parents (still skint) and Linn (now two) were living in a grotty and minuscule rented flat in Finsbury Park. The landlord didn't allow them to redecorate, and he also didn't allow children. The children thing, they could get around; every time he was due to visit, they'd frantically hide every toy and kiddy-sized pair of sandals under the bed, and Mum would take the evidence (item 1: Linn; item 2: her own growing tummy) around the block till the coast was clear. The other no-no was a bigger problem. Living in a house with walls that were decorated in depressing "mushroom", with furniture in shades of dull brown, dull-ish brown and *very* dull brown, just about sent my artistic mother round the bend. She told me she bought yards and yards of cheap sari material from the Indian shops up in Turnpike Lane and draped them over everything, but it didn't do much good. She said the only thing that cheered her up was looking through the bars of their basement-flat window at the rowan tree that dripped its red-berried branches over the neighbouring wall and into their bare little backyard. And so, Rowan got her name.

Next, things got a little better for my parents. Dad had worked in bike shops for years (the hardwork, pedal kind of bike, if you were wondering), when he heard about this old guy who was retiring and wanted someone to take over the lease of his small bike workshop in Crouch End. Cue, my dad. It wasn't too long after that that my folks spotted this genteely crumbling Victorian house around the corner from the workshop. Because it needed vats of work doing to it, it was dirt cheap, so they gave up their squashed rented flat for a big, falling-down house, all for the sake of their two small daughters and one big bump (me, Love Child No. 3). On the day they moved in, Mum took one look out of the front attic-bedroom window (my room) and copped a load of Alexandra Palace, and that sealed my fate. Alexandra Love is on my birth certificate, but my dad soon gave me the same nickname as my namesake: Ally Pally.

Three explanations down, one to go.

So, Dad had his business, and we had the house,

but my parents were still what can be technically described as skint. Because of that, the family tradition of camping holidays continued, and one rainy summer, when I was six, we found ourselves stomping up the slopes of Glastonbury Tor in Somerset. It's supposed to be this really mystical place (which, of course, is why my mother wanted to go), but I tell you, it doesn't feel too mystical when you're getting soaked by persistent heavy drizzle and your mum's stopping to throw up halfway to the top. But there you go. That holiday had its good points – well, one, anyway. Mum realised that Love Child No. 4 was on its way. And, in due course, there was a baby, and that baby was Tor (minus the Glastonbury bit, thank goodness).

Sandie loves the stories behind our names; she thinks they're terribly romantic. And you can't blame her. Her parents didn't exactly exert their imaginations when they came up with Sandra, which is what her mum is called too. She was thrilled when I accidentally called her "Sandie" once – after we'd just begun to get friendly last year, when we both first started at Palace Gates comp – and it's all she's let anyone call her ever since.

So, anyway, here we were in our hall – me, Dad, Sandie and two muddy-pawed dogs.

"I was taking a DVD back to the shop for my mum and dad," Sandie smiled, sticking her thumb back in the direction of the kitchen, where she must have left the disk. "Do you fancy watching it together this afternoon before I drop it off?"

"Yeah, OK," I said, trying to find space on the overcrowded coat-hooks to hang up my jacket. "What is it?"

It was funny, but right at that moment, just looking at Sandie, I got another flutter of that worrying feeling that I'd forgotten something...

"Don't know. It's something with Nicole Kidman in it, so it should be all right."

"Cool," I nodded.

Then I noticed Sandie was doing something weird with her eyes, making them go wide and then darting them to the side.

Normally, I'd say that Sandie's eyes were the nicest thing about her; they're blue and round and pretty, kind of like a character's out of a Disney movie. (Tor thinks her eyes are exactly like his rabbit Cilla's – and I guess he's got a point. She does tend to do that startled, bunny-in-headlights thing a lot.) But today, rolling them around like she was doing, she looked downright deranged.

Dad was still milling about between us, searching for his house keys and the set for the workshop, so

I guess she was trying to let me know something without alerting him. But what it could be, I hadn't a clue.

Looking slightly frustrated at my lack of psychic power in figuring out what she was on about, Sandie dumped her coffee cup down on the hall table and stomped up the stairs.

"Going to the loo," she said needlessly, stepping over a snoozing cat (not Colin) and throwing one of those bizarre boggly-eyed looks at me over her shoulder.

"OK," I shrugged, passing Dad as he pulled his coat on and giving him a peck on the cheek bye-bye.

Then, heading along the hall to the entrance to the kitchen, I suddenly remembered what Rowan had gone out for.

"Hey, Sandie!" I bellowed after her, loud as an alarmingly loud foghorn. "There's no toilet pap—"

It was then that I saw what Sandie was trying to signal with her eyes.

There, sitting at the kitchen table, gently brushing another cat (also not Colin) off the Sunday supplement in front of him, was Alfie.

Alfie.

With my mouth still hanging open where I'd forgotten to finish my sentence, I stood rigid in the kitchen doorway, wondering if it was possible to rewind my life by ten seconds so I wouldn't look and sound like such a dork.

"Hi, Ally..." he said, glancing up at me from the magazine he was – cat allowing – trying to flick through.

It was hardly even a glance – more of a glancette – but the merest eye contact with Alfie tended to have the most traumatic affect on me: I stopped speaking English and started to speak gibberish.

"Huh – uh, hi," I mumbled, stepping forward awkwardly into my own kitchen.

I was walking with these funny bobbing little moves, like an insecure chicken.

"Uh ... where – where's Linn, then?"

"Linn?" he repeated gently, like he was talking to someone who wasn't quite all there. Which I wasn't, in his presence. "I'm just waiting for her. She's on the phone, I think..."

Alfie looked back down at the magazine, which was perfect. It gave me a second to gaze at him, take in the gorgeousness of him, uninterrupted. His short, messily spiky blond hair; those spookily pale, grey eyes; that heart-bursting smile that stretches so wide you can sometimes see the gold tooth he has on one side; that cute leather strappy bracelet thing he wears round his wrist; those skinny but

38

muscular tanned arms... Hey, tell me when you've got an hour. I've only fancied him for ever, so the full list of his many charms tends to run on a bit.

"So," I squeaked, deciding that I should try and squeeze a conversation out of him while I had him all to myself. "What are you two ... guys up to to-to-today?"

For some reason I was stammering, which I never normally do. And for some reason, I'd adopted a faint transatlantic twang to my voice, and believe me, I don't make a habit of acting like an extra out of an American teen show too often either.

He gazed up at me, and I knew my face must be practically *luminous* pink. My cheeks felt so hot you could fry an egg on them. Except for the fact that it'd keep slipping off them, since I was standing...

Getting sidetracked by the logistics of the egg-frying stuff *might* sound insane, but believe me, having a mind that regularly wanders off on garbage like that really helps sometimes. Like right then – it distracted me from my total and utter fluster and I instantly felt the furnace in my face fade away.

"We're just going into town... Check out Carhartt and that in Covent Garden..."

He spoke in this slow drawl of his, which is *just* delicious. Course I didn't have a clue what he was on about, but I just nodded knowledgeably anyway. It had to be some trendy clothes shop; he was really into labels and stuff.

"Ah. Right. Well … um … don't do anything I wouldn't!"

OK, so *now* I knew I'd morphed into some seedy and deeply corny bloke off a building site. I could sense that this was *not* going too fantastically well, and I was considering faking a faint just to put an end to my agony when a blood-curdling scream erupted from somewhere upstairs.

Alfie looked shocked.

"What was that?" I yelped, turning and hurrying out into the hall, hoping the relief I felt at the diversion wasn't written *too* obviously all over my face. I mean, for all I knew, something truly terrible could have happened.

But of course it hadn't.

"Sandie!" I panted, after leaping up the stairs two at a time and staring into every room to find the source of the scream.

Sandie was sitting on the edge of Tor's bed, rigid with fear. If I thought her eyes were mad earlier, it was nothing on the I've-just-seen-an-alien! boggling they were doing now.

"What the hell—" barked Linn, appearing at my side, along with Alfie, who'd followed me up the stairs.

But it wasn't her stare or her gritted teeth that was the freakiest thing. It was the fact that, for some bizarre reason, Sandie had all these *twigs* in her hair.

And, uh-oh…

They were moving.

Chapter 5

ONE SURPRISE, WELL AND TRULY SCUPPERED...

"You shouldn't have done it."

"Why?"

"Because it wasn't nice."

"Why?"

"Because you scared her."

"Why?"

"Why *what*?"

It's hard having a conversation with Tor sometimes. As he's a boy of very little words, it sometimes gets kind of tiring trying to read between his (short) lines.

"Why was she scared of them?" Tor asked, gazing at me across the table, all doe-eyed confusion.

"*Because* when Sandie said she'd like to see them," Rowan explained, as she passed a plate under our little brother's nose, "she didn't think you were going to put the stick insects *on her head*."

Earlier in the afternoon, Linn, Alfie and I were still trying to figure out the best way of removing Tor's latest additions to the household from Sandie's hair

– with Tor anxiously watching and wailing at us not to damage their little stick legs – when Rowan came back from the corner shop. Luckily for the general health of the stick insects, she came up with the smart idea of wafting a lettuce leaf over Sandie's shaking head, enticing them away from the aroma of Head & Shoulders and up on to the safety of much healthier vegetation.

Now, his tea sitting untouched in front of him, Tor blinked and said nothing, but you could tell by the look on his face that he was highly disappointed in Sandie's reaction.

He's always deeply suspicious of anyone who doesn't display at least one hundred per cent adoration for animals*, and when he'd hijacked Sandie on her way to the loo to show off his new pets, the last thing he'd expected was for her to act like she did. (*The one exception to Tor's suspicion list is Grandma. She's not at all fond of the animals, but she's very fond of Tor. And Tor is very, *very* fond of his grandma.)

"Rowan, what exactly *is* this?" demanded Linn, staring at her plate in open disgust.

"Well, remember Dad said we should eat more fish…" said Rowan plaintively, her bracelets jangling as she sat down in her own seat.

She looked hurt, but I don't know why. Linn

always has a pop at her efforts every time it's Rowan's turn to cook, so you think she'd be used to it by now. Linn, Rowan and Dad take turns to cook at the weekend. Not Tor, thank God, or we'd probably end up with a tin of cat food, Hula Hoops and hamster mix. (Grandma comes round and cooks tea for us during the week, since us girls are all – ahem – busy with our homework.)

"Yeah, so we should eat more fish. But *this*?"

Linn wasn't being very nice, but then – if I'm honest – neither was our tea. Potato waffles, coleslaw and … kippers. I rest my case.

"Well, it was really busy in the fish shop yesterday and I just got a bit flustered!" Rowan tried to explain herself. "I just … panicked and pointed to the nearest thing when it was my turn!"

If you ask me, the reason she got flustered is 'cause there was quite a cute Saturday boy working in there.

"I'm sure it'll be lovely," Dad interrupted diplomatically. "Thanks, Rowan!"

Rowan gave Dad a grateful smile and reached over for the tomato sauce. Smart move – smothering everything (including coleslaw) in tomato sauce is just about the only way to get through one of Rowan's meals.

"So, Dad…" said Linn, gingerly picking at the

fish. "I was thinking, it's your birthday soon. And last year, we all went out for a pizza, didn't we? But this time round, why don't we stay home and cook something special here?"

"Will Rowan make it?" Tor piped up, with a panicky expression on his face.

"No. Definitely not," Linn reassured him, ignoring Rowan's disgruntled tutting.

My heart sank – I knew what Linn was up to. As far as she was concerned, the surprise party was All Systems Go, and making sure Dad didn't want to go out was just Phase One of her masterplan.

"Stay home? Fine by me," shrugged Dad. "You know I don't like a fuss."

See? I felt like yelling at her, *he doesn't like a fuss!*

And correct me if I'm wrong, but you don't get much more of a fuss than a surprise party.

"Speaking of fuss; poor Sandie," Dad laughed. "She must have been so embarrassed today."

He was right there. Poor Sandie. She's a total sweet pea – you'll never find anyone more trusting or kind – but on a one-to-ten shyness scale, Sandie's a nine-and-a-half, no problem, which makes me pretty protective of her actually. She was so traumatized by the stick-insect incident that she just spent the whole Nicole Kidman movie quietly groaning to herself; and even though I kept zapping the pause button and asking if she was OK, all she'd say was that she was fine. But put it this way, she kept covering her face with her hands so often, she couldn't have seen much of the film.

"Yes, she *was* pretty embarrassed," I nodded, wincing inside for her. I mean, *I* wouldn't exactly like to have someone cool like Alfie seeing me in such a total state.

"I can't blame her," my dad continued. "Being stuck in a room with everyone staring at you and *only* you – that's my idea of a nightmare, that is."

My hand froze as I lifted a forkful of fish to my mouth (well, any excuse not to eat it), and threw a glance over the table at Linn.

She'd gone momentarily rigid too.

I flicked my eyes across to Dad, who – unless I'd gone mad (possible) – gave me the tiniest of winks.

Did he know? Had he overheard somehow? Had he suddenly developed psychic powers and sussed out what Linn had in mind for him? Or was what he said just a timely fluke, and the wink was just a twitch?

I didn't know, and I didn't care. All I *did* know was that the stupid surprise-party idea was well and

truly dead.
  Long live the next idea.
  Whatever that was.

Chapter 6

HEY! LET'S BE FRIENDS! (NOT...)

I was bumbling along the road on my way to school, half expecting to hear the familiar cry of "Alllllllllleeeeeeeeeee! Wait for *meeeeeeeeeeeee*!" from Sandie, but it didn't come. We never plan to meet, it's just that we often do anyway. My sisters go to Palace Gates too, but we all go out of our way not to walk to school together. That would be *so* not cool – for any of us.

Since I was on my own, I guess I should have been doing something constructive with my thoughts – like dreaming up an amazing present for Dad, or maybe even trying to figure out what that I've-forgotten-something feeling I'd had all week-end was about – but instead, inevitably, I thought about Alfie.

More specifically, I was thinking for the millionth time how Linn could honestly be Just Good Friends with someone as totally, omigod beautiful as him. I've never been able to figure it out – what does she see when she looks at him? Doesn't she just want to pounce on him? But, you know, I don't think she does. I've studied her sometimes when she's with him and nope, there's not a trace, not a *hint* of attraction going on there at all.

Same goes for him (I'm glad to report). But that's not to say Linn isn't pretty; she is. (And don't I know it...)

She's more like Mum than the rest of us. She's got Mum's almost blonde-ish wavy hair – not that you can see the waves, since she religiously blow-dries it straight every day – and almond-shaped eyes. (And those perfect boobs, of course.) Me, Rowan and Tor all take after Dad: straight, brown hair and matching Malteser-brown eyes. Of course, the one thing that would make Linn really, *really* pretty is if she smiled more.

Yeah, like *that's* going to happen in a million years.

But with the Alfie and Linn thing, it's not as if I think a girl and a boy can't be friends – I've got Billy, after all. But then, Billy is just, well, *Billy*. And Alfie is just ... *phwoarghhhh*.

Anyhow, I headed into the yard at Palace Gates comp and over to the main entrance, feeling pretty happy after my Alfie daydreams, even though it was Monday morning and I had a whole five days worth of school gaping out in front of me.

And there was still five minutes till the first bell – five minutes to hog a radiator and drool over Alfie in the privacy of my mind.

Or maybe not.

"Ally? Can I have a word, please? My office – now."

It was Mrs Fisher, our Year Head. We got told at the beginning of the school year that we had to look on Mrs Fisher as a friend, as someone we could talk to if we had problems. You know – her door was always open, blah-de-blah.

As *if*.

It took just a couple of gullible pupils to test *that* theory out for the rest of us to know that if ever we had a problem, we'd be better off talking to the janitor, the school nurse, or a random passing stranger about it than Mrs Fisher. I don't know what side of herself she showed off to Mr Bashir the Headmaster to get him to think she had it in her to be this compassionate advisor, but it *sure* wasn't the side we got to see. When it came to irritants like us, she was from the "Don't be silly – pull yourself together!" school of non-sympathy.

Needless to say, my good mood evaporated mighty quick as I obediently and silently followed her along the corridor and up the stairs to her office.

"This," she said, sweeping her door open and wafting her hand impatiently at someone sitting in a chair, "is Kyra Davies. And this—"

She wafted her hand vaguely in my direction.

"—is Ally Love. Ally, Kyra has just joined the school today, and she's going to be in your form class – therefore, I've decided to assign you to look after her for her first week. Show her about. All right?"

All right? I suppose it was. At least I wasn't in some terrible trouble over something I had no memory of, like I'd dreaded when Mrs Fisher had first summoned me. But now the relief that I wasn't about to be hung, drawn and quartered for some unknown misdemeanour was over, I got my first proper look at who I was going to have to babysit.

And I wasn't sure if I liked her.

Kyra Davies was sitting slouched in the chair, an arm sprawled casually along the back of it. She was chewing gum with her mouth open, eyeing me up and down quite blatantly, like I was a sack of potatoes she was trying to guess the weight of.

I tried to brazen it out and stare back at her, but I'm not great at that kind of thing; I don't have the bottle to act that hard (since I'm about as hard as mashed potato). I did stare enough to decide that she was Mediterranean-looking, or something.

She was quite pretty – apart from her sticky-out ears that looked glaringly obvious because of the way she'd dragged her dark, curly hair back into a top-knot – but she had this really kind of arrogant manner.

"Well, what are you waiting for, girls?" Mrs Fisher frowned. "The bell just went. You'll be late for your History class, if you don't hurry."

Chop, chop, go, go – that was Mrs Fisher's duty done, as far as she was concerned.

Kyra languidly stood up, hoisting her bag on to her shoulder, and blasted a teeth-baring, obviously insincere smile in the Year Head's direction.

"Thank you *sooo* much, Mrs Fisher," she said in a saccharine-sweet voice just dripping with sarcasm.

"Goodbye, Kyra," muttered Mrs Fisher in response, shutting the door firmly behind us.

"What a frigid old cow!"

I couldn't believe Kyra had the nerve to say that so loud, and right outside Mrs Fisher's door. And I couldn't believe that I suddenly found myself jumping to Mrs Fisher's defence.

"She's all right," I shrugged, walking off in the direction of the History class and just presuming Kyra would follow.

"Not from where *I* was sitting," Kyra snorted, falling into step beside me.

Maybe with someone else I'd have agreed with them straight away, but there was just something about Kyra's cockiness that bugged me, somehow. She'd only been at Palace Gates five seconds and she was mouthing off her opinions. It was a bit much, if you see what I mean.

"So, when did you arrive in Crouch End, then?" I asked, trying to change the subject.

"Last week," she replied, yawning.

I mean, *yawning* – how rude is that?

"Do you like it?"

"Don't know. Looks a bit boring. I told my mum and dad that we should live in south London, not north London, if we were going to move here at all."

"Oh?" I answered through gritted teeth, stomping along the corridor faster.

I know it's crazy, but I really love where I live – I'm really proud of how green and leafy and historic it is, and how many cool shops there are, and how comfy and trendy it is at the same time.

"Yeah – Brixton's much more happening than *this* place."

I couldn't say anything for a second, I was too annoyed. But I tried; I'm not into being rude. Even if Kyra was.

"So whereabouts are you living?"

"Cranley Gardens. The place we're in is a pit."

"Uh-huh."

Cranley Gardens is the sort of place that the local estate agents go all poetic over. It's a "highly desirable turning", apparently, and the way they tell it, every house is "luxurious". But not Kyra's, it seemed. God, just how spoilt was this girl?

"Mmm. So where did you live before?" I asked, relieved to see the door to Miss Thomson's History class in the not-too-distant distance.

"Rye. It's this little place down in East Sussex."

"I know it. We visited once when I was little."

"Total dump, isn't it?"

"I thought it was nice," I found myself protesting. "All those old, cobbled streets…"

"Yeah? And boring as hell."

Everything was a dump or boring, as far as this girl was concerned. Her boredom was boring me already.

"How come you moved?" I asked, out of politeness rather than actually wanting to know the answer.

"We move a lot. My dad's an assistant bank manager. We get around," she yawned again.

"And your mum?" I asked, eyeing up the approaching doorway.

"She's a professional drinker."

I shot Kyra a shocked look, and her face broke

into a lazy grin.

"Only joking…" she sniggered.

What a horrible thing to joke about, I frowned to myself.

But then I guess I'm pretty super-sensitive about stuff to do with mums.

At last, the doorway to the bright, white classroom loomed large.

Everyone was still drifting in, shuffling noisily into their seats. Over by the window, Sandie was already sitting in our usual spot; she shot me a questioning look. From the back of the room, where Chloe and Jen and the others sat, I could practically feel their eyes boring into my head, wondering what the deal was with the new girl.

"Hello, Ally. So this must be Kyra?" smiled Miss Thomson.

"That's me!" trilled Kyra, *really* insincerely.

I groaned inside. Being facetious with Mrs Fisher was one thing, but Miss Thomson was something else. She's too nice and reasonable to muck around with. Actually, she's my favourite teacher at school.

"Right, let's see… Do you want to sit yourself here for the moment, Kyra, and I'll come and chat to you in a second?"

With an almighty sigh Kyra flopped down into

the seat at the desk that had been pointed out to her.

Miss Thomson gave me one of those looks that, like my dad's the night before, *could* have meant something and then again might not. But from where I was standing, her eyebrows definitely shot up and down, as if to say, "*She's* going to be a pain, isn't she?"

But that was me guessing. Or wishful thinking. What Miss Thomson *did* say kind of took me by surprise.

"So, Ally, I was just in the middle of asking Sandie how you're doing with your project."

Our project.

Oh. My. God.

You know that thing I'd forgotten? All of sudden, I hadn't forgotten it any more...

Chapter 7

MORE STRESS? YES, PLEASE!

I'm not mean. Honest I'm not. Well, OK, I've been known to be a *bit* mean to Billy, but that doesn't count. He knows I'm only joking.

Hopefully.

But that Kyra – I was sick to death of her by the end of the day. It was absolutely zero fun, having to drag her around every class, and hear her slagging off the school all the time. (I got a break at lunchtime – I went home to my own place, as usual, after pointing her in the direction of the dinner hall.)

The world according to Kyra went like this: all the teachers she'd met at Palace Gates so far were morons; she was too smart for most of her old teachers and that's why they didn't like her; everybody in her last school was a total nerd; all her old schools were trash, but our school beat them all; everything about Palace Gates was scuzzy, especially the toilets.

Big wow – the toilets! What was she expecting? Fake-fur-lined seats and toilet-paper monitors handing out individual sheets to everyone entering a cubicle? Get real.

But if I'm honest, Kyra was just an irritation. The *real* problem that was doing my head in was our history project, and the fact that me and Sandie had done precisely nothing about it.

"I can't believe it's come up so fast!" I moaned, as the two of us mooched miserably out of the school gates on this Monday afternoon.

Trying to keep up with homework was one thing; trying to cram a project we'd had six weeks to do into the remaining two weeks was something else.

"I know," nodded Sandie.

"I mean, where's the time gone?"

"I know," Sandie sympathized.

"It's a disaster – we haven't even thought of what we're going to do!" I whimpered.

"I know," Sandie agreed.

We'd been told about this joint Drama and History department project a couple of months back. To celebrate our school's fiftieth birthday, the Drama crew were going to be putting on a play for local primary schools, based around what Crouch End was like fifty years ago. Us lot in the History department had been split up and given different tasks to do: some were helping with research for the play itself, while others – like me and Sandie – were supposed to be coming up with fascinating visuals on a wide variety of subjects to a) decorate the hall outside the auditorium, and b) expand the minds of the visiting small primary kids.

Back when Miss Thomson first told us about it, it had seemed about a hundred kilometres into the future. But now... *uhhhhhhhhhh*.

"How could we have just forgotten about it?" I moaned, miserable at my own crapness. It was my leaving-homework-till-Sunday-night outlook to blame, I guess.

"Mmmm."

It slightly jarred that Sandie had stopped saying "I know". What was "Mmmm" supposed to mean?

"Mmmm?" I repeated, staring at my best friend.

"Well..." said Sandie sheepishly.

"Well?" I asked.

"Well ... *I* remembered."

"Remembered what?"

"Um, about the project..."

"You remembered about the *project*?!" I yelped. "All this *time*? Why didn't you *say* something?"

"I was waiting for you... I thought you were thinking up an idea!"

Sandie blinked at me with those blue, saucer-like eyes of hers.

She does this *all* the time – waits to see what I

think about something before she says or does anything. ("That girl's got no gumption!" my grandma said once, when Sandie was prannying about at my house as usual, saying, "Oh, I don't know! *You* decide!" when we were working out what movie to go and see at the Muswell Hill Odeon.)

I know what Grandma meant, but it's pretty hard to stay mad at Sandie. She's the kind of friend who's good to have around; she's got a brilliant sense of humour (even if she doesn't have the confidence to be funny herself), and she's so honest that she'll always tell you things straight (but she's also smart enough to know when to tell a little white lie – like saying I look fine when I have the biggest spot in the cosmiverse erupting on my chin).

But you know something? Just this once, I was *really* mad at Sandie. I couldn't help it; it could land us in real trouble. I mean, I know I was a doughball (double doughball) for forgetting about the project, but it was pretty stupid of Sandie not to have said anything about it earlier.

I suddenly felt a bit sick. It was all such a total disaster. Then, just when I thought the moment couldn't get any worse, I heard a sound that made my heart bounce off the pavement.

"Hi, guys," said Kyra, very casually strolling up beside us.

But she didn't fool me – she must have had to run to catch us up, 'cause there was no one behind us a minute ago when I looked back as we were crossing the road.

"Hi," I said half-heartedly. "So ... what did you make of your first day, then?"

"Bo-*rinnnnnnggggggggg*. That teacher, Mr Horse Arse—"

"Horace. Mr *Horace*," I corrected her, quickly.

I was well aware of what all the boys in our class called him. But we'd been taught by him for ages, and since Kyra had sat through one measly class with Mr Horse Ar—, uh, Mr Horace, it did seem kind of cheeky of her to get so casual with his nickname already.

"Yeah, whatever," shrugged Kyra. "Anyway Mr Whatshisname is a complete plonker. He's the worst so far."

I'd had it. If I heard one more whinge about our school and everything in it, I'd have to kill her.

"Um, don't you live over *that* way?" said Sandie tentatively, pointing at the other side of the road we'd just crossed.

I could have kissed my best mate then and there. For once Sandie wasn't just letting *me* do all the talking. And it was a fair point anyway – what *was* Kyra doing coming creeping after us when she lived in the opposite direction?

"I was just … going … to the post office."

No she wasn't. I heard that little hesitation in her voice, and saw her glancing ahead quickly to see where she could pretend to be heading for.

"Oh, right," said Sandie, giving me a quick nudge with her elbow. Looked like she'd sussed out Kyra's porky-pie too.

"Well, bye!" I said cheerily, as we approached the door of the post office.

"Yeah, bye. So I'll see you at the main entrance tomorrow, then, Ally?"

Deep gloom. Being Kyra's school babysitter for the week was just too annoying to contemplate.

"Uh-huh. See you tomorrow," I mumphed, forcing a half-hearted smile.

"God, what's she *like*?!" whispered Sandie, glancing behind to check that we weren't being followed again.

"Like the most pushy, irritating, whining person on the planet?" I suggested, loud enough for anyone in the vicinity – possibly even in the post office – to hear me.

OK, so now I had *three* things to stress over:

1) The fact that the wind was blowing through the vast, empty wilderness of my imagination every time I tried to come up with an idea for Dad's

birthday. At this rate, Linn would be trying to force Very Bad Plan No. 2 on us any second now. And I dreaded to think what *that* could be.

2) The wind was *also* blowing through the vast, empty wilderness of my imagination when I tried to think up some super-amazing idea for the History project too. Not that it had to be super-amazing. An averagely dull idea would have suited me fine by this late stage.

3) And I had this miserable feeling that Kyra was going to be a bit of a cling-on. I worried that she would try and tag along with me and Sandie as the only possible options open to her. After all, from what we'd seen (and heard) of her, people at school weren't exactly going to be queuing around the block to become big buddies with her.

I'd left Sandie a few streets back – both of us vowing to come up with some project ideas overnight (i.e. she'd wait and see what *I* came up with and then agree enthusiastically) – and was quite glad to see my familiar front door looming up in front of me.

Then, walking up the garden path, I heard raised voices coming from inside my house and wondered if I'd done something particularly awful in a past life to deserve such an annoying day.

"What's everyone yelling about?" I asked, stomping into the living room and taking everyone by surprise.

Tor was sitting cross-legged on the floor, petting a cat that wasn't Colin, while Rowan, Linn and Grandma were standing, hovering in a circle around him. From their body language, it looked like my sisters were in the middle of some strop, with Grandma acting as referee.

"Ally, dear, we are *not* yelling," said my gran, contradicting what was so clearly true. "We're just having a debate, that's all."

"OK," I said, chucking my school bag on the sofa and plonking myself down beside it. "So what's everyone debating about?"

"Dad's birthday," Linn replied snippily, settling herself down at the other end of our vast, squishy, old sofa.

It groaned gently as she did so, like a long, low fart, completely ruining her air of superior snottiness.

I threw a glare at Tor that said, "Don't you dare giggle at her – it'll make things worse!" But Tor was smart and knew that already; he'd yanked the black and white cat up into his arms so he could bury his face – and giggles – in it.

"Rowan has had this *stupid* idea," Linn began,

ignoring the sofa squelch, "that we should get Dad a session with a feng shui expert for his birthday!"

I glanced around our sunshine-yellow living room – at the old sofa and chairs with their throws, mounds of cushions and magazines and papers spilling off them, then at the fireplace, at the shelves and surfaces, all covered in pictures and ornaments and bric-a-brac and books and plants and candles ... a feng shui expert would walk in here and collapse with clutter-overload.

"I thought that would be right up your street, Linn," I suggested, suddenly remembering I'd forgotten to include assorted pets in the living room inventory. "Getting minimal and everything..."

"Minimal!" squeaked Rowan in alarm. "I thought feng shui people brought you luck by moving the furniture around a bit and sticking a couple of wind chimes up!"

Poor Rowan obviously hadn't swotted up on her suggestion properly. But then, speaking before she put her brain in gear was her speciality.

"I wouldn't mind *any* excuse to get this tip sorted out," sniffed Linn, gazing round the room dismissively, "but it's not exactly something Dad would be into, is it?"

And neither is a surprise party, I thought silently, finding myself irritated with Linn turning up her nose like that. After all, most of the paintings and bits of pottery in here was stuff Mum had made.

"Well, at least I tried to come up with something special," Rowan huffed, the bangles on her wrists jangling with irritation. "At least it's not *boring*, like Linn's idea!"

"Now, girls!" Grandma interrupted, holding a hand palm up in the direction of each of my sisters.

"So what was your idea?" I asked Linn, kicking off my school shoes as I talked.

"Go on! Tell her your idea and see if she falls asleep!" Rowan said stroppily.

"I thought maybe a watch – with a message engraved on the back," shrugged Linn, turning round on the sofa to face me and studiously ignoring Rowan.

"But he's already got a watch – the one Mum gave him," I replied automatically. After all, I couldn't see Dad parting with *that* in a hurry.

"*See?*"

"Enough, Rowan," muttered Grandma. "All this silly bickering over your dad; he would be very upset if he thought you girls were falling out over him."

Nobody said anything then – we all knew she was right.

"Anyway, I thought I might have a suggestion for

you," said Grandma, folding her arms across her chest.

"What?" I asked bluntly.

"Well, the most important thing to your dad is all of *you*," she began, now unfolding her arms long enough to point a finger at each of us in turn.

We waited wordlessly, all privately hoping Grandma was about to solve our problem for us.

"So, why don't you give him a family portrait of you four children? That photography shop on Crouch End Broadway always has *lovely* photos in the window of families they've snapped in their studio. They're—"

"Oh, Grandma, *no*!" exclaimed Rowan, looking as horrified as if the government had suddenly announced a ban on the year-round use of fairy lights. "Those posed photos are *awful*! They're *so* naff! All soft-focus and cheesy smiles!"

Grandma frowned at Rowan, then glanced round at the expressions on the rest of our faces.

Even Linn, who was Grandma's right-hand girl, couldn't hide the fact that she thought it was a deeply corny idea.

"Right! If you don't want to listen to my advice, then fine!" said Grandma sternly, turning and heading out the door. "I'd better get started on tea anyway..."

Uh-oh – major huff alert.

Grandma tells *us* lot off for bickering or sulking, but boy, can she do a mean teenage strop when she wants to....

Chapter 8

HACKED OFF...

A word of warning: never, *ever* try to cut your fringe when you're in a bad mood.

I gazed at my reflection in the toilet mirrors while a bunch of girls who were in the year below me charged about screaming and giggling about something or other in the background.

Hopefully, it wasn't my hair, but I couldn't have blamed them if it was. One single, solitary chunk of fringe was cut so high that a big, shiny patch of forehead positively *gleamed* at me in the mirror. My fringe would've looked better if I'd just let Tor's hamsters *gnaw* on it for a while.

You see, Grandma usually trims my hair for me – it's just past my shoulders, with a fringe, so it's not like I'm any challenge to a hairdresser – but last night, she was still huffing too much for me to ask for hair-snipping favours, so I did it myself. In fact, Grandma was huffing so much that she didn't even stay for tea with us like she normally does; as soon as Dad came in she was off, saying there was a programme on telly that she really wanted to catch, which sounded like a flimsy excuse to all of us. Not that any of us let on to Dad that there was a problem – that would have been giving the game away.

So, today, I could add a new dollop of stress to my stress mountain. I had a non-existent History project (no overnight miracles there), no idea about Dad's dumb birthday present, Kyra still bending my ear with her moaning between classes, and now there was Grandma going all grumpy on us.

Oh, and a hairdo from hell.

"No! Don't! No! *Nooooooo!*" shrieked the girls behind me. They were really irritating me – I felt like explaining that it was still possible to laugh without doing it at a level of decibels that burst eardrums. But I was just in a bad mood.

Back to Grandma: she might come over all strict and everything but, underneath, she's a total softie. She tuts and gripes a bit at the state of the house (her flat is like one of those show homes – not a crumb or a speck of dust to be seen. You see where Linn gets it from...), but she's always been there for us. Well, especially since Mum and everything. A couple of years back, she even sold her house up in Barnet and moved to a flat round the corner from us, just to help out more. So even if she was a bit serious and not exactly the kind of person you could kid around with, there's no way I – or any of us – would deliberately want to hurt her feelings. But it looked like we'd managed to...

"Come on! That's the bell! Quick! A prefect might come in an' catch us!"

I moved my eyes away from the vision of hacked hair in front of me in the mirror, and watched the posse of giggly girls tear out of the loos.

I couldn't resist it. I had to have a nosey at what they were all in a tizz about. They'd seemed to be hovering around the cubicle behind me; I stepped across the scuffed vinyl floor and peered in.

Their art teacher wouldn't exactly have been proud of what they'd been doodling on the wall in thick black marker pen. (*I* certainly don't remember any diagrams like that from the sex-education talks Mrs Fisher gave us.) And their English teacher wouldn't have been impressed with the sort of stuff they'd been writing either. I mean, if you're going to scrawl obscenities on the toilet walls, you should at least spell them properly, shouldn't you?

"Nicole is a hoe," I read aloud. "A '*hoe*'?"

Not much of an insult, is it? Comparing a person to something that sits next to the spade in a garden shed, I mean.

But staring at the handiwork of a bunch of girls without a brain cell between them, it did suddenly occur to me that Kyra was right for once: the toilets at Palace Gates *were* pretty scuzzy.

Thinking of Kyra, I breathed a sigh of relief. I'd managed to shake her off at the beginning of the afternoon break, fifteen minutes before, and hadn't seen her since. Could it be that she was as bored as *I* was of us trailing around together? Could it be that at least one of my stress-factors was finished with?

I gave my hair a quick, useless ruffle in the mirror, and hurried out into the corridor.

Where I bumped slap, bang into Miss Thomson, my History teacher.

"Ally!" smiled Miss Thomson. "I've just been talking about you!"

"Oh?" I replied, wondering what was coming next.

"Yes – remember that you told me yesterday in class that you and Sandie were a little behind with your project?"

A little behind? Try four weeks behind...

"Well, I just had a surprise visit at the beginning of breaktime – from someone who could lend you a hand..."

I didn't have to listen as Miss Thomson finished what she had to say. All I knew was that me and

Sandie had just found ourselves with a little helper that we most definitely didn't want.

Kyra "in-yer-face" Davies.

Chapter 9

SMART IDEAS, WORSE LUCK...

A cat that wasn't Colin started sniffing at the tuna sandwich I'd just made.

"Oi!" I yelped, rushing back from the fridge with a bottle of low-fat salad cream in my hand (it had a "Property of Linn Love" sticker on it, but I was doing my best to ignore that).

The cat that wasn't Colin jumped off the work surface and walked indignantly across the wooden kitchen floor with a clickety-click of its claws. I peered after it, and saw from the funny bend in its tail that it was Frankie. That's the only way I can identify the cats that aren't Colin; by the broken bits on them. Tor, of course, knows every cat by the sound of its purr or the flick of a whisker, but it's harder for the rest of us. It's just that, apart from Colin (being ginger and having only the three legs), our other four cats are all a universal black and white. From a distance, or when they're snoozing in a tight cat-curl, it's hard to tell the difference. Up close, it's easier: Frankie has the wonky tail, Eddie has ears that are so fight-chewed they look like they're lace-edged, Derek is very cross-eyed, and Fluffy makes Frankie look good – he's got no tail at all.

"Your house is amazing! I love all the colours, and all the pictures and stuff!"

I didn't particularly like Kyra, I *definitely* resented having to include her in mine and Sandie's (invisible) History project, and I wasn't exactly *thrilled* at the idea of having to invite her back to my place this Wednesday lunchtime so we could go over our "plans" for the project.

But, hey, I'm shallow enough to appreciate a compliment when it comes my way.

"Thanks," I nodded, handing her a plate with a tuna sandwich on it.

The one Frankie had been sniffing at, of course.

Kyra pulled out the nearest chair, which was directly opposite Sandie, who was already halfway through her sandwich and had been flicking through a mag while Kyra was upstairs in the loo.

"Listen," said Kyra, peeling back the top slice of bread to inspect what I'd given her, "what's going on in the room at the end of the hall upstairs? I heard all these *noises*..."

I hesitated for a second as I blobbed a dollop of Linn's personal low-fat salad cream on my own sandwich, and tried to figure out what she meant. And then I realized – Tor's bedroom is a den of tanks filled with fish, stick insects, lizards and a variety of small things whirring round in wheels.

"Was it squeaking and scrabbling type noises?" I asked.

"Yeah!"

"That's my brother's hamsters and stuff."

"Wow – and you've got those two dogs too?"

Rolf and Winslet had been very excited by the sudden activity in the middle of the day. Normally it was just me and Rowan who were home at lunchtime (me, 'cause I like the peace, and Rowan 'cause – to be honest – she hasn't got any friends at school to hang out with in the dinner hall).

"Yes, and we've got five cats too," I said, yanking out another chair from the long wooden kitchen table and settling myself down.

"Yeah?"

I half-expected Kyra to come out with a sarky comment about smelly animals or something, but she didn't. I was surprised. But not as surprised as what she said next.

"So who's the freak-show sitting in your living room?"

I twitched. How dare she speak about Rowan like that? Although – as much as I didn't want to –

I had to acknowledge (only to myself) that Rowan *had* gone for a very odd look today. She'd twisted her dark hair into all these tight little bobbles on her head, like Björk used to do (which was weird enough as it was), and then tied tiny pieces of ribbon around each bobble. It must have taken her ages to do, and to be honest, the effect wasn't quite worth it.

Still, that *was* a member of my family she was talking about.

"That's her sister!" said Sandie, leaping to mine and Rowan's defence in the face of Kyra's tact-free comment.

"Yeah? Poor you!" snorted Kyra.

I was just about to throw a very sarky comment Kyra's way (if I'd been able to think of one fast enough) when she went all gooey all of a sudden.

"*Oooooh*! *Babe*eeeeeeee! What happened to you?"

From nowhere, Colin hopped up happily into her welcoming arms and set up a rattling purr that would have rocked the foundations of the house … well, in my dreams anyway.

"You mean his leg?" I said, obviously. "He had an argument with a car, and lost."

"Oh, my God, you must have been so upset!" Kyra exclaimed, stroking an ultra-content Colin.

"Nah, it happened before we got him," I shrugged.

"We inherited him from a friend of a friend of my gran's – they were moving away and couldn't take him."

But then that was the story of all our pets' lives; every one of them was wonky and shop-soiled in one way or another. Like Winslet; apart from her old-lady grumpiness, we also realized when we found two sets of keys, a hairbrush, a hot-water bottle and Dad's favourite jersey hidden under the doggy blanket in her bed that her kleptomaniac tendencies had probably helped lead her to be abandoned in the first place.

And the cats; well – apart from Colin – we inherited Frankie and Derek from nearby neighbours who'd moved in for four months and done a runner in the night, abandoning their four-legged furrballs, while Eddie had just been a stray we'd started feeding. Fluffy is the bad-tempered, feline equivalent of Winslet, who'd had her tail amputated after it was bitten by the Doberman she lived with. In the circumstances, Fluffy and the Doberman couldn't live together any more and, rather unfairly, their owners (people who worked in the grocer's next to Dad's workshop) decided that Fluffy should get herself a new home. Which happened to be ours.

"You're so lucky," murmured Kyra, nuzzling

Colin's head with her nose. "We've moved around so much we've never been able to have any pets…"

I sneaked a look at Sandie, who was sneaking a look back in my direction. If I read her mind right, I knew she was thinking, "What's with *her*?" – same as me.

It was hard to keep up with Kyra's changes of character. In the two and a half days we'd known her at school, she'd been the Snarl Queen. In the five minutes we'd been sitting in the kitchen, she gone from praising my house, to dissing my sister, to practically drooling over my cat and getting embarrassingly slushy over animals in general.

"So, this project," I said, trying to drag Kyra's attention away from Colin before she stroked the fur off his back. "To be honest, we haven't got very far with it."

"Oh?" said Kyra, gazing up at me.

"We haven't done, well, *anything*," Sandie shrugged, nervously scraping her fine, fair hair back behind her ears.

She had little pink spots of guilt on her cheeks too, I noticed.

It's not Miss Thomson we're having a tuna sandwich with! I felt like saying to her. *What are you blushing for?*

"Good!" exclaimed Kyra, puzzlingly.

"Don't mind me..." Rowan's voice drifted into the kitchen. She padded over to the fridge and was about to help herself to some orange juice when her hand hovered over a carton of raspberry yoghurt drink, which she picked out instead. It had a "Property of Linn Love" sticker on it, I noticed.

"Why's that good?" I asked Kyra, turning my attention back to her.

"'Cause I've had this brilliant idea!" she replied. "Well, it's a rip-off of something I did at one of my old schools, but I think it'll work OK."

"Go on..." said Sandie, leaning her elbows on the table and narrowing her big, blue, Disney eyes at Kyra.

"Well, you've got a local historical society here, haven't you? It's just that I bet they'll have maps about where bombs fell in this area during World War Two," explained Kyra, still busily fondling Colin's ears. "At my old school, we did these big posters, showing where the bombs fell, and showing photos from the time, with arrows and stuff pinpointing them on the maps."

"That sounds brilliant!" said Rowan suddenly, a pink yoghurt moustache noticeable on her upper lip. "People are always nosey about stuff like that, aren't they? Trying to see if the street *they* live on was affected!"

"Exactly!" agreed Kyra.

I looked from one to the other. Weren't they both forgetting something?

"Er, hello? Remember us?" I waved at my sister. "Thanks, Rowan, but it's up to me and Sandie to say if it's a good idea or not."

"Well, you haven't *got* an idea, have you? So you haven't got much choice," said Rowan curtly, looking a little hurt.

But then I felt a little hurt myself, with her having a dig at me. As if I didn't feel useless enough when it came to the project.

I watched as Rowan stomped out of the kitchen, back to the strains of some Aussie soap starting up on the telly in the living room.

I sighed to myself. If there's one thing I really hate it's when people are right about something you wish they weren't right about. If you see what I mean.

"So, what do you think?" asked Kyra.

"Mmm," I nodded reluctantly. "Sounds good. Let's do it."

Well, let's face it – it was do Kyra's idea or leave the country before Miss Thomson found out the truth...

Chapter 10

ALL THAT GLITTERS (IS IN ROWAN'S ROOM)

You know that Friday feeling? When it's like you've been set free for a whole, delicious weekend, starting as soon as you get out of the school gates at four?

Well, I didn't have it. Or at least I had it for fifteen whole minutes, till I got home in time to see Rowan storming up the stairs, hiccuping with tears, while Linn was shouting, "Oh, for God's sake, Ro, stop being such a baby!"

"What's wrong now?" I asked Linn, following her back into the living room.

"Ask *her*! I was just trying to have a discussion, and she flounces off. As usual."

Linn flopped down on the sofa and picked up a copy of some magazine. From the way she was holding it up in front of her face and angrily flicking the pages, I could tell I wasn't going to get any more out of her.

I turned and walked out of the room, into the hall – its lilac walls looking more bruised purple as the strange stormy light poured in through the glass panels on the front door – and headed into the kitchen.

"I'm keeping out of it," said Grandma, anticipating what I was going to say.

Beside her at the kitchen table was Tor, sucking unhygienically at the end of his pencil, a notebook with scrawled sums open in front of him.

"But, Grandma, what are they—"

"Ally – Tor and I are too busy doing his homework to worry what silly girls are arguing about. Aren't we, Tor?"

My little brother nodded.

"And silly girls like that would be better off getting *their* homework out of the way on a Friday afternoon instead of bickering, wouldn't they, Tor?"

Tor nodded at Grandma again and looked back down at his sums.

Compared to his sisters, Tor might have been in Grandma's good books for now, but he wasn't all sweetness and light. I could see the slight bulge in the top pocket of his school shirt, and I could see it was moving. Since it was only a small pocket, I guessed that one of his white mice must have been chosen to come down and be his maths muse. If Grandma spotted that she would *not* be amused.

If Linn and Grandma weren't going to tell me anything, then there was only one person who would. And she was upstairs snivelling.

"Rowan?" I said softly, knocking at her door.

There was no reply.

"Ro – it's me, Ally!" I called a little louder, in case she thought it was Linn coming to continue their fight, whatever it was about.

"Mnnnumph!"

I took the trumpeting of her nose to be a yes, and walked in.

It was only twenty past four and shouldn't have been so dark outside, but the purply-orange storm clouds lay low and ominous outside the big bay window. Because it was as if twilight had landed early, Rowan had already switched on her collection of fairy lights and charity-shop lamps. With all her trinkets twinkling in shades of pink and green, red and yellow, the effect was beautiful. Her whole room was beautiful, in an over-the-top, brain-dazzling way. Everything was beautiful – except for the hunched-up girl perched on the bed, her mascara smeared and her nose immersed in a snotty white tissue.

"That's new," I said, pointing to a kind of collage thing on the wall.

It was a sugar-pink fluffy heart mounted on a big

piece of baby-blue art board. All round the edge of the board and the heart, multi-coloured sequins were glued, and in the centre of the fluffy heart itself was a tiny doll, wearing what looked like a little tutu.

"I made it last weekend," sniffed Rowan, blowing her nose again. "Found the doll in a junk shop on Saturday and decided to do something with it."

She seemed a bit happier already – talking about the pictures and stuff she made always cheered her up. Linn maybe got Mum's looks, but Rowan definitely got our mother's love of all things arty-farty. Me, I didn't inherit either Mum's blondey-fair hair or her arty-fartyness. I don't know if I inherited any of her traits at all, really; sometimes my memory of her is a bit hazy. Which is a pretty weird feeling...

"Nice," I commented, though I wasn't sure if I'd have fancied something like that up on my wall.

"Thank you," said Rowan, uncurling her legs from under her and starting to look more composed.

"So, what were you and our lovely big sister arguing about?" I asked, lowering myself down into her green blow-up chair. It was on the semi-deflated side – my bum was just about touching the floor – but it was still kind of fun to sit in.

"Oh, her!" sighed Rowan, throwing a theatrical

glare at the ceiling. "Linnhe is so bossy it makes my blood fizz!"

Now if I was Linn, I'd have been correcting her at that point, telling her the word she was looking for was "boil", not "fizz". But I didn't bother – that's just the sort of thing that Rowan comes out with and I always find it quite entertaining. My favourite thing is when she's singing along to the radio in the shower or the bath – she warbles along really enthusiastically, but *always* gets the words wrong.

"What's she bossing you about for?" I quizzed her.

"You'll never believe it," said Rowan, her eyes wide and comical with all the black mascara smeared round them. "She's only just gone and decided that this family photo of Grandma's is a good idea after all!"

"What?" I yelped, nearly bobbing out of the inflatable plastic chair in surprise. "How come?"

Rowan flopped back on to her squashy rose-covered duvet.

"That's what I tried to ask – before she bit my head off!"

"What did she say?"

"She said that since me and you hadn't bothered coming up with anything, Grandma's idea was probably the best we were going to get and we

86

should just go for it."

I felt a twinge of guilt at that. Like with the History project, I'd been spectacularly bad in the inspiration department.

"Then I tried to say that I didn't want to do it," Rowan continued, "and Linnhe tells me to shut up unless I had something useful to say!"

I couldn't see Rowan's face at that point, since she was lying on her bed and I was practically down at carpet level, but I could tell she was going all snivelly on me again.

"Don't let her get to you!" I said lamely, as I struggled to get out of the wobbly seat.

There was only one thing for it, I decided: I had to try to come up with a better idea for a birthday present before Linn went and booked an appointment at the photographer's. Linn and Rowan were going to come to blows soon if things went on the way they were, and I didn't suppose Dad would be all that chuffed with a grinning portrait of his family, with his two oldest daughters showing off the black eyes they'd given each other.

Speaking of Dad...

"Hey, Ally Pally! Come to make sure your old dad gets home safely?"

Dad had stuck his head out of the back workshop at the sound of the bell above the door, and I squelched my way in, trailing wet footprints across the lino.

"Well, you're always reading about old people getting mugged in the street these days..." I grinned at him.

An oily rag came whizzing in my direction.

"What did I say?" I jokingly protested, ducking sideways and letting it fly clean past me.

"Give me a minute – I'll wash my hands and then I'll be ready," he called out, disappearing further into the workshop. "The rain's really hammering down out there now, isn't it?"

"Yep. So, been busy today?" I yelled above the sound of running water in the sink.

"Not really," he yelled back. "Pretty quiet for a Friday. I sold one kid's bike though."

Dad didn't just repair bikes, he sold second-hand ones too – in the teeny-tiny front shop I was now standing in, dripping.

"So, what's brought you round here, Ally Pally?" Dad's voice drifted through.

"Don't know – just felt like a walk," I shrugged to myself.

What a joke. If I'd wanted a walk I'd have grabbed Winslet and Rolf and gone up to the Palace or to Queen's Woods – not just tootled five minutes around the corner to Dad's shop. And moseying out for a stroll isn't the first thing you generally think of doing when a storm's just broken and the rain's bouncing in sheets off the pavement.

No, I didn't just fancy a walk: unknown to Dad, I was on a spying mission...

"So," said Dad, appearing in his red checked shirt and jeans in the doorway of the workshop, drying his hands with a towel, "you haven't come round to pick my brains about what I want for my birthday?"

Damn. Guess the FBI wouldn't be calling to recruit me soon.

"How did you know?" I asked, slouching in defeat.

"Oh, I overheard Linn talking to Rowan about it last week," he grinned at me. "Tell me, Linn's not still keen on that surprise-party idea, is she?"

"No," I reassured him, remembering that look I thought he'd thrown me across the kitchen table a few days before. "You managed to put her off on Sunday, when we were talking about Sandie and what had happened with the stick insects."

"Good," he smiled, chucking the towel over an old stool and pulling his worn denim jacket off the hook on the door. "I don't want any big fuss. I'm just happy to have all of you guys – I don't want anything fancy."

It was one of those lump-in-the-throat moments. I knew he was thinking of the one person who was missing from the equation, and *he* knew that *I* knew what he was thinking. I blinked hard and tried to say something funny before I started the waterworks like Rowan.

"Don't let on to the others, but keep an eye on things, will you, Ally?" said Dad, sliding his taut, muscular arms into his jacket.

"Sure," I gulped, still feeling that lump in my throat, especially now that Dad had trusted me with his thoughts.

"Maybe you could try not to let things get out of hand," he continued, patting me on the shoulder.

"No problem," I reassured him. "So, no fanfares; no cheerleaders; no ticker-tape parades..."

"Exactly!" laughed Dad, coming and putting his arm around my shoulders and ushering me out the front door.

OK – so now I knew what he *didn't* want. But it still hadn't got me any closer to figuring out what he *did* want...

Chapter 11

CHEEK, AND PLENTY OF IT...

"Ally – look!"

Now, Tor isn't one of those annoying kids that goes loopy in toy shops. You know, the type that just start grabbing anything within a metre radius, whining "Can I have this? Can I have this? Can I have this? Can I have this?" over and over again like a jumping CD.

Nope. I can safely say that I could take Tor into the best toy shop in the world, and he wouldn't twitch. But take him to the local pet shop, and that's a different kettle of gerbils altogether...

"Ally – it's pretty isn't it?"

Tor's brown eyes were gazing up hopefully into mine. We were here at the pet shop doing our regular Saturday-morning stint, stocking up on hamster bedding, fish food and whatever little extras Tor managed to wangle out of our budget.

"Uh, yeah, I suppose it's quite pretty," I nodded, peering at the small sponge ball covered in soft, glittery, tinsel spikes. It looked like a strange mating between a hedgehog and a Christmas decoration. "What is it?"

"Cat toy," said Tor earnestly, pointing at the display box full of glitter-spiked balls he'd plucked it from.

"Mmm. Looks more like a Rowan toy," I commented, thinking how much our sister would like something that sheeny-shiny and stupid.

Tor giggled.

It's great having a kid brother sometimes; it doesn't matter *how* lousy your jokes are, they always laugh.

"Better not tell her about these, Tor," I said to him, all mock-serious. "She'll be in here buying the whole lot, and end up glueing them round her headboard or something."

Tor giggled some more. And then he stopped.

"Can I get one, then?" he blinked up at me. "Please?"

He doesn't miss a trick; really he doesn't.

There he was, luring me into a false sense of security, pretending he thought what I was saying was funny and everything, and then *wham* – just when my guard's down, he hits me with the wide-eyed pretty-pleases.

"Well, if we buy this, then we can't go for a hot chocolate…" I warned him.

That's part of our Saturday-morning ritual too –
going for a hot chocolate at Shufda's, a little egg 'n'
chips caff a couple of doors up from the pet shop.
Unless, of course, we end up spending our "treat"
money on stuff like sponge glitter balls.

"That's OK," he shrugged. "The cats'll like it."

So, we headed home early, armed with pet bits
and cat toys. With just me and him and no one else
around, I felt it was time to pick Love Child No.
4's brain.

"You heard Rowan and Linn fighting yesterday,
didn't you?" I asked, as we trudged along the busy
pavements, sharing a consolation Kit Kat (well,
even if we didn't get our hot chocolate, we still had
to keep our sugar levels up...).

"Yep," said Tor, leaning sideways with the weight
of his shopping bag.

"It didn't upset you, did it?"

"No."

"Did you figure out that they were arguing about
what to get Dad for his birthday?"

"Yep."

"So, what do you think, Tor? Do you think
Dad would like a big framed picture of the four
of us?"

"Nope."

93

Like I say, he's a boy of few words. But you always get his drift pretty easily.

"What do you think *would* be a good present for Dad, then?"

Tor looked up at me, his eyes squinting against the sun.

"The zoo…"

"The zoo? Well, I know we want to get Dad something good, Tor, but I don't think even all our pocket money clubbed together is enough to buy the whole of London Zoo…"

"No!" he said, whacking me on the arm with his half of the Kit Kat. "A day out! All of us! And Grandma!"

Ooh, I could just see Grandma there, pulling a disapproving face at the sight of the baboons and their obscenely red bums. Or Linn yawning and looking at her watch. And considering Dad had taken Tor to the zoo one Sunday last month, I didn't think he'd particularly think it was some big-wow birthday treat to go and count the penguins yet again, quite so soon.

"Right, fine. Thanks, Tor – that's, er, another idea to think about!" I lied, as we took the turning into our road.

"Who's that?"

Tor was pointing his chocolate bar into the

distance.

"Who's that where?" I asked, peering down the street to see what he could see.

"At our door," said Tor, now nibbling distractedly at his Kit Kat, like one of his hamsters let loose on a carrot.

Fleetingly, I just made out a figure – a dark-haired girl – being let in our front door.

"Wasn't that Von?" I suggested.

Von is one of Rowan's best buddies; one of her two best mates (the other one is a monosyllabic guy called Chazza) who our gran strongly disapproves of. Mainly because they're quite a bit older than my fifteen-year-old sister (Von and Chazza are both eighteen) and pierced (in Von's case it's her nose, in Chazza's it's his eyebrow), and because Grandma really has a thing against nicknames (Von is short for the hard-to-get-your-head-around Irish name Siobhan, Chazza is playground mumbo-jumbo for Charles). Can you imagine my uptight grandma giving it the old "So, how are you ... Chazza?" It doesn't come naturally, I'll tell you that. But what choice does poor old Rowan have? All the people in her year give her a pretty hard time, since they think she's so weird and everything, so if Von and Chazza think she's cool, who cares if they're older, pierced, or in possession of rubbish nicknames?

"No – it wasn't Von," Tor said definitely.

"Was it one of Linn's mates?" I suggested, wracking my brain. "Mary? Or maybe Nadia?"

"No."

I frowned. Who was wandering about in our house right now? If that girl wasn't one of Linn or Rowan's mates, then who was she?

"She had big ears," said Tor simply.

He's a bit spooky sometimes, my brother (no wonder Billy calls him Spook Kid). He has this thing where he hones in on details other people just don't get...

"You couldn't have seen her ears from all this distance away!" I laughed, as we trudged along the pavement.

But as soon as the words were out of my mouth, I remembered someone who did have big ears, when her hair was pulled back tight in a ponytail.

It suddenly occurred to me who the girl in my house really was. And she wasn't a friend of *mine*.

The cheek of Kyra Davies...

Chapter 12

WHOSE HOUSE IS IT ANYWAY?

Rowan was sitting at the table, her knees tucked up inside her white, cotton, Victorian-style nightie. From where me and Tor were standing in the kitchen doorway, it made her look like she had enormous matronly bosoms.

She was still sleepy from her long lie-in – you could tell by the way she was yawning and the way her hair was sticking up at one side. Lucky for her, someone was filling the kettle to make her a cup of coffee.

"Oh, hi! I just got here," said Kyra, ever so casually, as she plugged the kettle in. "I woke Rowan up ringing the doorbell, so I'm making her a coffee to make up for it. Do you want one?"

It's weird seeing someone you don't know or like very much making themselves at home and rummaging about in your kitchen cupboards for mugs. Not just weird; downright INFURIATING!

"Uh, Kyra – wasn't I meant to phone you later, about meeting up?" I said, hoping she'd get my point.

She didn't.

"Oh, it's no problem," she shrugged, clattering cups down on the work surface. "I've already been to the Historical Society – I've got everything we'll need."

Now, you see what I mean about the girl? How presumptuous was that? The plan was supposed to be that I'd call Sandie and Kyra around lunchtime, and work out a time to go to the Historical Society *together*, so we could research and pick out all our reference stuff for the project *together* ... and now look what she'd gone and done. She obviously had some kind of difficulty understanding what "together" is supposed to mean. Like, it doesn't mean "Never mind anyone else; you just go on and do whatever you fancy..."

I was so mad, I couldn't think what to say.

"Yeah, I got up early this morning and was just a bit bored," Kyra blithely continued, turning and placing a cup in front of Rowan.

"Thanks," muttered Rowan sleepily.

"No problem. So I thought I might as well go along and get everything we needed. What do you take in your coffee, Ally?"

I still hadn't said anything, and I was still hovering uselessly in the doorway, carrier bags in hand.

"She takes milk. And one sugar," yawned Rowan, doing my talking for me.

"Well, are you going to sit down?"

I'm an idiot sometimes, I really am. This bossy, pushy girl tells me to sit down in my own house, and what do I do?

I sit down.

"Look, this is what I got," Kyra continued, settling herself into a chair and pulling copies of photos and maps out of a white plastic bag. "All we need to do is get these blown up to poster-size first – does the office at school have a good photocopier, or are we going to have to go to a specialist copying place?"

"I ... I don't know," I shrugged stupidly.

"Oh, wow – look! This is Von's street!" said Rowan, suddenly springing to life at the sight of the first photo on the pile.

"Yeah – see this house here? It's completely gone. That's where the bomb fell," Kyra explained.

"Gee, this is going to be really interesting for everyone, seeing if their street was bombed..." mused Rowan, riffling through the other photos. "This must have taken you for ever to sort out!"

"Yes, it did. But the two women down at the Historical Society were brilliant, helping me go through everything."

Do you ever get times where you feel surplus to

requirements? That's how I felt right then, watching my sister and this practical stranger sitting with their heads together, cooing over *my* project.

And it was about to get worse.

"Do you like hamsters?" said a small voice.

Because I'd been so stunned at the sight of Kyra Davies swanning round my house like she was my lifelong buddy, I hadn't noticed Tor disappearing from my side. And I hadn't noticed him reappearing, sidling up to Kyra with a handful of fur, teeth and claws.

"Yes I do!" said Kyra, turning and attempting to stroke Mad Max.

"Don't – he bites!" warned Tor.

Too right Mad Max bites. Tor had inherited him a few weeks earlier from the reception class at his school. Instead of being this sweet, fluffy creature for the little kids to cuddle and love, it turned out that Mad Max was the Rottweiler of the small-mammal world, merrily biting children and teachers at every possible opportunity. If Tor hadn't taken him, Mad Max was destined for a one-way trip to the vet...

I got quite chirpy at that point. Tor was testing Kyra; forcing her to come face to face with his scariest pet, and see how she'd react. Good lad.

"He won't bite me!" said Kyra assuredly, scooping

Mad Max right out of Tor's hand and cuddling him to her chest.

Come on, Max, I thought to myself. *Do your stuff!*

"Prrp! Eeeeee!"

"He likes you!" chirped Tor, grinning in delight.

Great.

I couldn't even trust a hamster to be on my side...

Chapter 13

KISSING BILLY (YEAH – LIKE, RIGHT!)

The grass was a little bit too damp to lie on, but I didn't care.

Staring straight up, I watched little, ripply clouds wisp their way across the blue, blue sky. Then, accompanied by a far-away roar, a large plane came streaming over the top of Alexandra Palace, its silvery wings glinting with reflected sunlight.

I love skywatching. It chills me right out. Whenever my head gets in a knot, or if I just fancy a daydream, I come and flop down here at the top of the hill and gaze into space. The best part is when the planes swoosh past though – I love imagining who's sitting up there, eating free peanuts, as they gaze down on the amazing aerial view of Ally Pally (the building) and maybe the less impressive and much smaller Ally Pally (me) – if their eyesight's sharp enough. I always wonder where they're going and what their lives are like...

That Sunday morning, I'd happily have swapped places with anyone on the big silvery plane up above me. It wasn't as if anything dramatically *bad* was happening in my life, but I *was* feeling well and truly fed up by how irritating and complicated things can get.

Like the business of Kyra turning up unannounced the day before, and half my family falling for her. I tell you, I'd decided that it was the *last* time I'd take Rowan's side over Linn's, and the *last* time I'd go shopping for spoilt cat toys with Tor...

If only I was on that plane, going somewhere far away... I wished to myself, watching it fly off towards the horizon. *Anywhere that wasn't here would do...*

You know how some people have recurring dreams? Well, I have a recurring fantasy. It goes like this: I'm sitting on a plane that's headed for somewhere tropical and warm and beachy (this week's choice of imaginary destination was Sri Lanka – I'd seen it on a travel show and checked out where in the world it was on the big map on my bedroom wall). Anyhow, I'm on this plane, gazing out of the window at these great, fat clouds below me, when someone asks if I'd mind them sitting in the empty seat next to me. And my heart skips a beat or three, 'cause I recognize that slow, lazy drawl, and I turn round to find Alfie, smiling his gold-toothed smile at me...

Good fantasy, isn't it? Lying up there on the hill, I often try to edge it on a little further than that; you know, start imagining me and him hanging out on the beach together at whatever's my Destination of the Week, rubbing SPF15 on each other's bodies… But somehow, I don't tend to get that far. Mainly because – back in the real world – Winslet will end up padding over and licking my face, just to check I'm not dead or anything. Or Rolf will come and drop a drool-covered plastic disk on my tummy, so that I know that I'm neglecting my Frisbee-chucking duties.

"Yip! Yip! Yip! Yip!"

Winslet had just finished slobbering her dog-food-scented tongue all over my mouth and nose, when I heard her growling at the incoming dog.

"Hi!" said Billy, staring down at me, and blocking out the sun with his back-to-front baseball-capped head. (The baseball cap was back-to-front, not his head. Though with Billy, it's hard to tell sometimes.)

"Out of the way," I replied, motioning him to move over. "I'm trying to beam myself on board that plane, but your big head's between it and me."

Billy lifted his hand to shield his eyes and stared into the sky.

"What – *that* one?" he asked, pointing to the plane as it headed into the distance, above the skyline of central London.

"Yep," I nodded, pushing myself up on to my elbows.

Further down from us on the grassy slopes, Precious was doing his level best to shove his precious nose exactly where my dogs didn't want it.

"What do you want to be on that plane for?" asked Billy.

"I'm bored of the petty irritations that make up my life," I moaned. "I want that plane to take me away to somewhere exotic…"

"What, Gatwick airport?"

"Huh?" I blinked at him.

"Well, with *that* flight path, and at *that* height, I'd say it's about to land at Gatwick airport," said Billy, crouching down beside me.

Billy doesn't have a romantic bone in his body, he really doesn't. Which is another reason he doesn't have a girlfriend. I mean, I'm not saying he was wrong; it's just that he never knows when a girl doesn't want to hear cold hard facts about flight paths and unglamorous local airports and needs some sympathy and understanding instead.

"Anyway, I don't know what you're on about –

you've never even *been* on a plane," he pointed out unkindly. "You don't even know if you'd like it."

"So?" I answered defensively.

But he was right. It's just kind of embarrassing sometimes to admit that your family can't afford to take you on flash holidays. I'm not knocking the camping stuff we've always done (well, I *do* when it rains…), but it can still make you feel like you're missing out compared to other people.

"You all right?" he asked, suddenly noticing my grumpy expression.

"No."

"What is it – your hair?"

I'd tried to brush my fringe into some kind of side parting, but it obviously hadn't covered up my hack job.

"No," I protested, running my fingers through it again, like it would help.

Ha.

"So what's up, then?"

I sighed at the grating memory of Kyra getting cosy in our kitchen with Tor over a packet of milk-chocolate Hobnobs.

"There's this new girl who's started at school this week – and I might end up having to strangle her with my bare hands."

"How come?" frowned Billy, pulling his cap

round the right way. "If she's annoying, why don't you just ignore her?"

"Ignore her? Huh!" I snorted. "That's kind of hard, when she's already been helping herself to tea and biscuits at my house!"

I didn't want to ruin another day of my weekend by talking about Kyra, but you know how it is – you have to have a moan. And Billy is quite good to moan to, and knows me better than most. I guess I'm closest to Sandie, because she's a girl and because we go to the same school, but like I said before, Billy's my oldest friend.

We got to know each other when our mums took us to the same playgroup. I liked Billy straight away because he was the only kid who was willing to let me bury him in the sand pit. (He's a very trusting soul.) Oddly enough, my mum and his got to be pretty good friends too. It was odd because his mum's this real neat fiend, who dresses in matching shoes and handbag just to go to Tesco's, whereas Mum was more of a long, baggy skirt and hand-knitted jumper kind of person. And when we were small, Billy's mum would be all uptight, bleaching and disinfecting every surface and every toy in case a stray germ dared to infect her precious little boy, while my mum horrified her by claiming that if everyone licked the kitchen floor each day we'd all be so toughened against germs that we'd never need antibiotics. (We never did though. Lick the kitchen floor, that is.)

Although I played round there a lot when I was small, I don't much like going round to Billy's house now – his mum always gives me these really pitying looks and asks how we're all coping...

Anyhow, that day, Billy ended up sitting on the grass beside me just long enough to hear my whinge about Kyra and to get a wet bum, courtesy of the damp grass.

"And what's she like in class?" he asked, once he'd got the whole story.

"She does that thing where she's totally cheeky to teachers," I explained, "but she does it so subtly, they can't get her for it."

"Like how?"

"Well, you know – they'll ask her a question, and she'll tell them the right answer, but with this really *boooorrred* tone in her voice. Or say 'Yes, *Sir*' or 'Yes, *Miss*' but with this *sneer* in her voice."

"I'd love to meet her."

You could have knocked me down with a sparrow's feather then. After everything I'd said, after explaining how my family seemed to be taken in by her, Billy'd let me down. His girl radar had gone up, and he'd blanked out all the bad bits I'd told him.

"What?!" I yelped.

"Well, I'd like to meet her – just so I could snub her. Show her she's no big deal."

Right then, I could have put my arms around my best mate Billy and given him a great, big kiss.

If the idea wasn't so totally icky.

Chapter 14

GOOD VIBES AND BIG MOUTHS...

"You know, I think it's growing in already," Sandie lied sweetly.

I knew it was just Sandie telling one of her occasional morale-boosting white lies – bless her – so I didn't bother to contradict her, even though my reflection was telling me something radically different.

I rifled around in my bag for the butterfly clips I knew were in there somewhere. My fringe was going to get clamped off my face until it had reached a decent length to be seen in public again.

The reason I decided not to tell my friend that I knew she was spinning me a line was that I'd made a decision; and that was to stop being a moany git.

After I'd seen Billy the day before and sounded off all my woes to him, I'd gone home and idled the rest of my Sunday away, mooching around miserably. There was nothing worth watching on telly in the evening, so I decided to stomp upstairs to my room and dig out my most depressing CD to listen to. But as soon as I walked into my room, before my hand automatically went to flick on the light switch, I saw out in the dark night the glowing vision of Alexandra Palace (don't worry – it wasn't on fire again).

Normally, as soon as darkness falls, you can hardly make the Palace out, but now, all lit up at the top of the hill, it almost looked like it was some fantasy fairytale castle, floating in mid-air. Spotlights shone the length of the Palace's yellow brickwork, the stained glass of the vast Rose window was illuminated like a giant version of something you'd find eating up the electricity bill in Rowan's room, while white streaks of lasers whizzed from the parapets up into the night sky.

OK, so I knew that the Palace must have all lights blazing because they were holding some big corporate do there, but even if this magical apparition was down to the Chartered Surveyors Annual Chartering and Surveying Awards or whatever, the startling prettiness of it still shook me out of the rotten mood I'd been slithering into all week.

Suddenly, I realized that being grumpy was boring me to death.

From tomorrow, I vowed, kneeling on a chair and staring off at the stunning sight of Ally Pally, *I will stop whingeing and whining, and be calm and positive. Hopefully...*

So, here I was, being calm (etc.) first thing on Monday morning, standing outside the main entrance to school, and about to explain my new approach to problems (i.e. Kyra) to my best mate (i.e. Sandie).

"You know something, Sandie?" I said, struggling to get my butterfly clips to stay put.

"What?" Sandie replied, holding up her pocket mirror so I could see what I was doing.

"We shouldn't let this stuff with Kyra wind us up," I mumbled, holding a purple clip between my teeth.

"Yeah?"

"Yes. I've been thinking: we can't get out of doing this project with her, so I think we should just ... grin and bear it and make the best of it."

"Oh, OK," nodded Sandie. "And I suppose we've got to feel sorry for her too. Being new and everything..."

See? Sandie always tries to be nice. But sometimes she's *too* nice. Well, she's a lot nicer than *me*, anyway. I was still grumpy with Kyra for doing all that stuff without us on Saturday.

"But Ally..."

Uh-oh – was I wrong? Was Sandie going to have a bit of a moan about Kyra?

"What?"

"Well, I'm confused…"

"What about?"

"Uh, does that mean we are going to be proper friends with her … or not?"

"No, it doesn't mean we have to be *friends* with her," I tried to explain. "It just means that me and you are mature enough to work with her for the next week without any hassle – and then once the project and the play and everything's out of the way, we start trying to shake her off. Gently."

"Oh, OK – I get it," nodded Sandie.

While we'd been talking (and hairstyling), the area around the main entrance had started filling up, full of people like us who were dawdling around, chatting, delaying till the very last moment taking that first Monday morning step into the school buildings.

"Hi, Ally, hi Sandie…"

It was Chloe Brennan, along with Salma and Jen and Kellie. They're like my second-division mates, after Sandie and Billy.

"Not hanging out with your new best friend, then?" Chloe grinned at me.

I like Chloe, but she's a bit mouthy, a bit cheeky

sometimes. Sometimes she winds me up, if you want to know the truth. And twenty-four hours before – when I was feeling all bitter and spiky – that dig of hers would have really bugged me. But now I was calm and serene, and no digs about Kyra Davies were going to get to me.

"No – I just had to show her around for her first week. Thank God."

Oops, that came out a bit spiky and not too serene.

Must try harder...

"She's a real show-off, that Kyra, isn't she?" said Salma, yawning.

You'd like Salma; she's got this laid-back way about her – as if her natural habitat is lazing on one of those posh, slinky chaise-longues sofas, doing nothing more energetic than chatting to mates down the phone all day. Sometimes the things she says would sound sarky coming out of anyone else's mouth, but when she says stuff, you know she's only trying to be funny.

"Yeah, she's got a right attitude on her. Did you hear her in French class the other day?" chipped in Kellie.

Kellie's cool, but she's a total gossip queen.

"Oh, yeah!" Jen giggled. "She started arguing with Mr Matthews, didn't she, when he tried to correct her pronunciation!"

Jen's a real giggler – she does it at the most out-of-order moments, like in assembly, or when there's a sad, slushy, romantic moment in a movie.

"It's like she wants to be the centre of attention all the time, isn't it?" Salma commented. "Silly cow..."

Ouch. Maybe Salma wasn't just being funny, for once. Still, at least, it wasn't *me* who was being bitchy. Even if I couldn't help smiling.

"Oh, hey, Ally – did you know that new horror movie's out this week?" said Chloe, suddenly changing the subject.

I knew what was coming next. Chloe is very popular within our little crowd – her dad runs this grocery shop that does a sideline in DVD rentals, and every time a new movie comes out that we want to see, Chloe can always get her hands on it a couple of days before it's officially meant to go on the shelves. And then that's where *I* come in – all of us take turns having everyone over for a girlie DVD night once in a while, and it looked like right now, it was my turn to turf the family out of the living room and let my friends invade.

"Cool," I nodded. "Do you want to come over at the weekend to watch it?"

"Nah – it's got to go out on the shelves on Friday, so we'll have to do it before then."

It's stupid, I know, but it's a bit of a buzz for all of us, getting to see something before anyone else, so I had to come up with a better offer.

"OK, Wednesday, then?"

They all murmured and ummed and ahhed, but eventually everyone settled on Wednesday being film night.

BRRRRRRIIIIIIIIIINNNNNNGGGG!!!

Big mistake – we were standing right under the bell.

"Fantastic!" I grinned inanely at Sandie once the shrill sound had faded. "The start of a whole new week at school! I don't know about you, but there's nowhere *I'd* rather be!"

Sandie grinned back, knowing exactly how I felt. That is, about as pleased as if someone had suggested superglueing my eyelids together...

Me and Sandie had just turned to follow Chloe and the others up the couple of steps to the main entrance, when I felt this weird sensation, like a stare was burning into my head.

I flicked my eyes to one side, and across a crush of people I caught sight of Kyra, hurriedly averting her gaze to the tarmac. Strangely, in that split-second, I noticed her ears – not 'cause they were big (that goes without saying) but because they looked deep pink against her light-brown skin.

("Ah! Ears burning – it's a sure sign someone's talking about you!" Grandma's words rattled round my head. She's very matter-of-fact, my gran, but she still likes to trot out ye olde worlde superstitious sayings from time to time.)

Urgh, I thought, my heart suddenly sinking with guilt. Was Kyra standing anywhere near us while everyone was talking about her? Had she heard?

Call me a hypocrite, but I hated the idea that she might have caught any of that, and got hurt by it.

Ally Love – you are a hypocrite.

There, I've said it myself.

Chapter 15

SISTERLY LOVE (DON'T LAUGH...)

"No! Don't you dare!"

At Linn's barked command, Rowan stopped dead, her hand hovering over the saucepan on the cooker.

"But it needs it!" whimpered Rowan. "It'll be really boring on its own!"

"Spaghetti bolognese does *not* need curry powder!"

"But—"

Rowan was a braver girl than me (and madder – I mean, curried spaghetti bolognese?). Linn was looking particularly frosty-faced, and arguing with her when she was wearing that expression was just pure insanity.

"Ally – *tell* her, before I ram this spoon down her throat!" Linn beseeched me, waving a tomato-sauce-stained wooden spoon ominously in the air.

"Um," I muttered, hovering in the kitchen doorway.

Both Linn and Rowan were staring at me, waiting for my verdict.

I wished Grandma had been able to make the tea as usual, instead of having to pootle off early to get ready for a someone's wedding-anniversary party this Tuesday night (partying on a Tuesday night? Our gran had a better social life than us...). Then there wouldn't be a battle for cooking supremacy going on between my two sisters, and I wouldn't be stuck in the middle as an unwilling referee.

"I think..." I said slowly, stalling for time. "I think curry is *brilliant*; but I quite like spaghetti bolognese just the normal way."

There – was that tactful enough to satisfy them both?

Nope.

"You *told* Ally to say that, Linnhe!" Rowan burst out.

"*When?*" gasped Linn, laughing at Rowan's plainly ridiculous accusation. "You mean, when I sent her an extra-sensory, telepathic message as she was walking through the hall two seconds ago? Oh yeah, you are *so* right, Ro!"

"There you go – twisting everything round so you look like you're *so* smart!" Rowan snapped at her, blinking hard like she might be on the verge of tears.

"Yeah? Well, looking smart's not hard, when I'm anywhere near *you*..."

"Shhh!" I hushed them, wide-eyed. From where I was standing, I'd heard the telltale creak of the stairs, even if they didn't.

Linn suddenly turned her attention to stirring the spaghetti, while Rowan grabbed the sponge by the sink and started wiping the work surface.

"Mmm, that smells good," smiled Dad, walking into the kitchen. "Anyone seen my specs? I'm supposed to be helping Tor with his homework, but it might help if I could read what the heck he's supposed to be doing…"

"Oh, they're here, Dad!" said Rowan cheerfully, handing Dad the glasses he'd left lying on top of the breadbin.

"Thanks, Ro. So, you girls all right?"

I knew then that he'd heard the raised voices on his way downstairs from Tor's room.

Me and my sisters, we've got this unspoken rule: never to let Dad catch us arguing. It's not fair to him, you see. He's had such a rough time with what happened with Mum and everything, that he would just get really flipped out if he thought we were ever falling out with each other. So, rows, bickering, disputes ("Debates", as Grandma would say), whatever; they're all kept well away from Dad.

"Yes, we're fine!" I said, probably a little too

brightly to be convincing. "Those two were just moaning a bit because I was reminding them I've got my mates coming round tomorrow night!"

"Oh, Ally – don't be silly! You know me and Rowan don't mind!" smiled Linn, playing the part.

She's very good at pretending her and Rowan get on. The only time she lets her true feelings show in front of Dad is when she's confronted by Rowan's terrible attempts at cooking on her nights in charge of the kitchen. But, well, people do have their limits...

"Yeah! I was just reminding Ally that she better remember to tidy up when they've gone – last time her mates came round, Rolf and Winslet were eating spilt popcorn off the floor for weeks! Weren't they, Ally!"

Rowan was positively twittering now. She's a born actress, she really is. Over-acting a speciality.

"Good. Anyway, I better get back up to those multiplication tables!" smiled Dad, as he pushed his specs on.

The three of us girls stood like statues, stupid grins fixed on our faces, till we heard Dad clomp back up the stairs and listened to the creak of him opening and shutting the door to Tor's room.

Then World War Three started again.

"You are so *bossy*, Linnhe! You think you can tell

all of us what to do and think!" Rowan hissed.

She was furious with our eldest sister, that was for sure, but considering she had done her hair in these two stubby short plaits, Rowan looked more like she should be going out to milk the cow in an ancient episode of *Little House on the Prairie* than arguing over curry powder in the middle of a kitchen in Crouch End.

"What's this got to do with anything?! What are you having a go at me for?" barked Linn, her green eyes blazing. "And for the ten thousandth time, my name is *Linn*, not *Linnhe*!"

"For one thing, you – you still want us to do this stupid family-portrait thing, even though me and Ally and Tor think it's a totally rubbish idea," Rowan railed at her. "And another thing, you can change it as much as you want – you can say you're name's *Bob* if you want – it doesn't change the fact that Mum gave you the name Linnhe, and that's who you are!"

It went strangely silent again at that point. Linn looked weird at the mention of Mum, like she'd been slapped in the face or something. Rowan looked upset at being forced to bring it up.

I didn't feel too good either, being reminded of the big, yawning gap in our lives. But I remember that Dad once said that your brain has an amazing capacity for protecting you from pain. And right at that moment, my brain obviously decided that it was going to distract me from sad, longing thoughts of Mum by giving me the giggles.

Suddenly, I found myself just struggling not to laugh out loud at the idea of Linn being called Bob...

"If you *must* know," Linn said huffily, pulling herself together and turning her attention back to her stirring, "I don't think we *should* do the family-photo thing now..."

A cat that wasn't Colin swooped round my ankles, alerted by the smell of cooking.

"Why not?" I asked, picking up the battered black and white moggy and identifying it by its crossed eyes as Derek. "I thought you were dead keen on the idea."

Linn pursed her lips.

"That was before I found out how much it costs..." she mumbled finally.

Ah-ha, so *that* explained her frosty features.

Rowan had a triumphant little grin on her face. She was about to say something that would end up with both my sisters yelling at each other again, I could tell.

"How much *would* it cost?" I leapt in, before Rowan could.

"More than we could afford," Linn said firmly.

Rowan was itching to speak.

"OK," I said a little too loudly, anticipating a vindictive outburst from our in-between sister. "So let's think of something else, then…"

"Like what? You haven't come out with any useful suggestions so far!" Linn said to me, pointedly.

Derek was wriggling to be free. He could sense the sisterly tension in the room and, smell of food or not, he was keen to be out of the kitchen and cuddling up somewhere more chilled-out.

"Well, why don't we all go to Camden Market this weekend?" I suggested, letting Derek bounce down on to the floor. "If we can't find something unusual for Dad there, then we'll never find it anywhere."

I don't know if you've ever been to Camden Market, but it's absolutely amazing. It started off years ago as a little patch of stalls in some old buildings by the canal in Camden and it's been expanding ever since, taking over every dilapidated old factory and building in the area. The stalls sell weird, wonderful and bizarre stuff, from clothes to food (OK, so neither of those sound particularly bizarre, but you haven't seen what some of them are like), to clocks carved out of driftwood, knitted pot-plant ornaments and wind chimes made out of old forks. Weird, I know, but good. Trust me.

Linn and Rowan glanced briefly at each other. Without saying anything, it seemed like something had been decided.

"OK," nodded Linn, for both of them. "Let's go to Camden at the weekend."

Phew.

I'd stopped them rowing.

Even if it just meant they'd be saving their worst quarrels for when they tore each other's hair out at the market on Saturday.

Still, Camden Market's so full of buskers and street entertainers that people might watch Linn and Rowan fighting and just presume it was performance art.

I could stick a hat in front of the two of them and see if any tourists chucked money into it…

Chapter 16

OH, THE HORROR...

"Present for you!" giggled Jen, standing on my doorstep.

"Jen! It's fabulous! You shouldn't have!" I fooled around, taking the tube of Pringles she was holding out towards me. "Come on in – everyone's here already."

Letting her close the front door behind her, I zoomed back into the living room and leapt into the one free armchair.

"Hey, where am I supposed to sit?" Jen protested, looking around at us all.

Chloe had bagsied the beanbag and was lolling on the floor, while Salma and Kellie were both stretched out, at either end of the sofa, like Siamese bookends.

Sandie, meanwhile, was sitting scrunched up to one side of the other armchair from me, looking not entirely comfortable. Rolf's gangly-limbed, furry body took up the rest of the space, his head lounging, *very* comfortably, in Sandie's lap.

Jen stuck her bottom lip out and did a very passable impression of someone who was three years old and about to have a major blub.

A Wotsit came flying through the air and hit her on the face.

"Oi!" she yelped, and took a dive at Kellie – the Wotsit-chucking culprit – tickling her mercilessly till Kellie had wriggled over enough to leave a reasonable gap on the sofa between herself and a cackling Salma.

Jen spotted the space and jubilantly parked her bum there.

At the same time, Rolf – sensing food on the loose – bounded off the chair he was sharing with Sandie and gave chase to the rogue crisp, utilizing her stomach as a handy launchpad.

"Rolf!" I snapped at him, as Sandie grimaced at the sudden impact of a dog diving off her abdomen.

"No, it's all right! I'm OK!" gasped Sandie breathlessly, waving one hand in the air and trying to smile.

She hates "being a bother", as she calls it. If she'd been playing the Drew Barrymore part in the film *Scream*, she'd be lying in a pool of blood at the end of the scene whispering, "No, I'm fine. Honestly! It's just a scratch!"

"Right, chuck me the disc, then, Chloe, and I'll

get the movie on," I said, pushing myself off the chair and kneeling down by the DVD player. "So, how scary is this one meant to be?"

"Worse than the *Blair Witch Project*, my dad says," Chloe replied. "But wait a minute, Ally – you never answered my question."

"What question?"

My mind was a bit of a muddle; it had been all go since I finished school for the afternoon. First I'd had to go shopping and buy enough crisps, dips and Coke to keep my mates happy for the evening, then I'd had to stop my family from eating or drinking any of it before my friends actually arrived. And despite the fact that my dad is very fair about us all getting a "turn" to have the living room to ourselves like this every once in a while, it had still been a nightmare to shoo them all out before Sandie and Chloe and the others rang the doorbell.

"Before Jen arrived – I was asking about Kyra, remember?" said Chloe. "How it's going with her and the History project?"

Urgh. *That*.

It was all right for Chloe, Jen, Kellie and Salma. Right at the start, they'd been excused from doing anything for the History project, because they'd offered their services in the make-up and wardrobe departments for the play itself. Cushy, if you ask

128

me. Whereas me and Sandie, we had to endure Kyra at close quarters, spending our History lessons stuck exclusively with her and our pile of posters. The Drama group were performing their play starting on Monday, so it was all hands on deck to get everything finished; which is why Miss Thomson had given us class time – and a note to our other teachers to let us have the whole of Friday afternoon off – to get everything finished.

"It's going … all right," I shrugged non-committally, without catching Sandie's eyes. I knew she'd be thinking I couldn't be telling less of the truth. "But, hey, let's not speak about boring stuff like that. Let's get the movie on!"

"Aw, come on, Ally," said Kellie. "Spill! We already told you how much she was bugging us today in Mr Matthews's class, when she started putting on that stupid over-the-top 'haw-he-haw' French accent."

"Oh my God, yeah!" Jen half-gasped, half-giggled. "Was she taking the mick out of Mr Matthews by doing that, or did she genuinely think he'd be impressed with it or something?"

"Come on, Al," Chloe cajoled me. "You and Sandie have seen more of her than we have. You've even had to put up with her coming round here to work on your project, haven't you? So what's going on with that girl? Is she a big-head, or is she just totally mad, or what?"

"Listen, I can't really be bothered talking about her," I mumbled.

I also didn't want to give up on my own personal resolution not to moan.

"Oooh, are you getting all protective of her?" Kellie sniggered. "Is Kyra your new best friend, then?"

"*Her*? You *must* be joking!" I barked. "I'd rather clean the loos at school with my toothbrush than be friends with Kyra Davies!"

So much for my resolution.

"Who are you whinging on about now, Ally?"

Linn stood in the living room door, looking at me in her best snooty and superior older-sister manner.

God, you know, it *really* bugs me when Linn does stuff like that. For one thing, I thought she'd gone out already (Rowan was upstairs in her room listening to music and creating her next junk masterpiece, while Dad and Tor were doing some father and son bonding, watching a repeat of *ET* together on the old portable telly up in Dad's bedroom). For another thing, Linn always seemed to save that snooty and superior older-sister malarkey for when my friends came round. And most annoying of all, it was easy for her to make a glib comment when *she* hadn't had to spend the last few days in enforced close contact with Kyra Davies, getting told "No, Ally, that photocopy's too blurry. Do it again" and "Give those scissors to me, Ally, you're not cutting it straight" and "Don't tint that photo that colour, it looks crap!"

And I'd been good and patient and non-moany, just like I'd promised myself, even though Little Miss Know-It-All was working my nerves so much that she was in danger of finding her *face* getting photocopied.

"I'm not whinging, I'm debating," I tried to say calmly, borrowing that favourite saying of Grandma's.

"Yeah! Like, *right*!" snorted Linn, pulling her jacket on.

I suddenly had a vision of my perfectly featured sister with *her* nose squashed sideways on a photo-copier too.

It made me feel marginally better.

"That'll be Alfie..." Linn muttered out loud to herself, as the doorbell shrilled.

My tongue was totally tied and I could feel that my face was about one million degrees hot – partly through my anger at Linn sounding off and showing me up in front of my friends, and partly because

131

Alfie was in the vicinity…

Then I found myself distracted and infinitely cheered up by the sight of Chloe pulling a face and silently mimicking my sister's nagging. But she soon stopped *that* in a hurry as Linn reappeared in the living-room doorway.

"Another one of your lot," she announced, before breezing off.

Sandie, Jen, Chloe, Kellie, Salma … there wasn't any more of "our lot" to come.

"Hi. I haven't missed the start, have I?"

Six mouths fell open at the sight of Kyra Davies and her bare-faced cheek.

Chapter 17

I HATE HER, I HATE HER NOT...

The young guy with the naff blond-dyed hair job was *not* having a good day. First, he'd fallen out with his girlfriend, *then* he'd gone round to her flat to apologize, only to find that she wasn't up for listening (mainly because she was a tiny bit dead). And now – thanks to the neighbourhood's local friendly axe murderer – Blond Bloke was wearing most of his insides on the outside. And *boy*, that wasn't a good look.

Normally, with horror movies, I'm a total wuss – I watch them from behind cushions, like that'll protect me or something. But this night, I ended up watching the random delights of gore, suspense and more gore with the sort of blank indifference I usually save for the gardening shows my dad regularly tunes in to.

Of course, it wasn't blank indifference I was feeling; it was complete shock. Kyra turning up like that – as if she'd been *asked*, for God's sake – was just so mind-blowingly cheeky that I didn't know what to say to her. Obviously, she must have overheard us all talking about having a girlie film night the other morning outside school, and just … well … decided to include herself in the invite.

You know what I said when she asked if she'd missed the start of the movie? OK, before you guess, here's a random selection of things I *should* have said. If I was the kind of girl to have the bottle. Which I'm not.

1) "What gives you the right to turn up here just like this, Kyra? You're *bang* out of order…"

2) "Missed the start? You're going to miss the whole movie, girl. Turn round and leave where you came in…"

3) "*Hellooooo?* Earth calling Kyra! Let me explain: down here in the *real* world we have this cute little custom where we actually *invite* people to come to our houses, not just have them turning up on our doorsteps like *psychos*!"

See, any of those – though not very nice – would, in the circumstances, have been reasonable responses.

But, oh no; Kyra Davies turns up unannounced at my house (for the second time) and, in answer to her question "Have I missed the start?" I faff about and say, "Umm … no", then watch helplessly as she gazes around the room and settles herself on the floor, leaning her back up against the chair Sandie's sitting on.

"Brought these!" she'd said, opening a white plastic carrier bag and chucking several bags of tortilla chips, kettle crisps and dry roasted peanuts on to the coffee table where the other bowls of nibbles already sat.

Everyone was too stunned to say anything – maybe, since it was my house, they were waiting for me to blast off at her, but I didn't.

Instead, I – oh, the shame – told her to help herself to the two-litre bottle of Coke perched on the table, and immediately pressed play on the remote.

The plot of the movie hadn't even sunk into my frazzled brain, when suddenly a wizened hand burst out of the ground, where the landslide had put an end to the terrible reign of the axe murderer by burying him in choking mud (except it hadn't – you could sniff a sequel coming a mile off).

"What a load of *pants*!" snorted Kyra, as the credits rolled up.

It was a typical Kyra comment, at least from what I knew of her from the last couple of weeks. It didn't make it appropriate though.

"Excuse me?" Chloe bristled, staring across the carpet at Kyra.

Since the DVD was from Chloe's dad's shop, and it was her little kick to give us the treat of seeing it before any paying customers, she wasn't too thrilled with criticism.

"Come on, it *was*!" protested Kyra, wide-eyed.

In one hand, she held a mound of popcorn; in the other, a full glass of orange juice; and in her lap was a snoozing cat that wasn't Colin.

"And you're some fancy film-critic, are you?" snarled Chloe.

"Don't have to be," shrugged Kyra. "Any moron could see that that was pants. I mean, that bit when the girl feels sorry for the killer and starts singing him a lullaby – no wonder he ripped her head off!"

Actually, you know something? The film *was* pants.

Kyra had the judgement to see that. Sadly, she didn't have the judgement to see that she was getting so far up the noses of everyone in the room that she'd need a native guide to get her back out...

"And that bit when the blond guy saw his girlfriend splattered round the room – couldn't he have at least *tried* to act like he cared a bit more? I mean, has he even *been* to drama school, or did he just walk into that part off the street?" Kyra continued her critique, ramming some popcorn in her mouth after she'd made her point.

"Are you for *real*?" Salma suddenly asked, with this really disgusted look on her face.

OK, so now you're seeing the other side of laid-back Salma. She's quite pretty – she's part Portuguese, or Brazilian or something, I forget – but when she's really hacked off, you'd think from the look on her face that she absolutely despises you. But she doesn't – it's just a momentary thing and it's just the way her face is.

Kyra wasn't to know that. But while anyone else would have spotted Salma's expression and shut up, Kyra didn't seem to notice and went merrily on...

"And the guy's mum!" Kyra carried on, regardless. "Were we really supposed to believe—"

"Erm," interrupted Jen, staring her small, but intense eyes like a shoot-to-kill laser beam at Kyra. "Do you want to shut up for five seconds?"

And for once, Jen *wasn't* giggling.

"What?" said Kyra, furrowing her brow. "Aren't I allowed to have an opinion?"

I felt these prickles at the back of my neck. This was getting really uncomfortable. I was starting to wish I'd never bothered having this film night. I could tell the others were staring at me, expecting me to say something, but I just couldn't think what.

"Well, you *might* have been allowed to have an opinion – *if* I'd invited you here tonight," I suddenly heard myself squeaking.

"Yeah, tell her, Al!" Kellie encouraged me, clapping her hands together.

"What's this got to do with *you*?" Kyra snapped at her. "It's not *your* house, Kellie!"

"No – it's Ally's!" Chloe barged in to the conversation again. "And she didn't ask *you* here tonight, did you Ally?"

I looked across at Chloe, perched forward agitatedly on the beanbag, and nodded, feeling a trickle of sweat tickle its way down my forehead. God, I really *hated* when things got all, y'know, *prickly*.

And it was about to get even *more* prickly...

"What's this got to do with you, Ginger Nut?" snapped Kyra.

Ouch. Double ouch. Chloe didn't mind if you called her a redhead, or auburn or copper or whatever other attractive name you find on the side of hair-tint boxes to describe her natural hair colour.

But start in with the ginger jibes, and you were dead.

"Tell me something," said Chloe, leaning

ominously close to Kyra, her almost transparent white skin even more blanched than usual, "were you born mean, or did you have to practise for a really long time?"

Kyra stopped chewing on her popcorn and stared at Chloe.

Something had hit home.

A split-second later, Kyra scrambled to her feet – surprising the cat that wasn't Colin from his slumber and out of her lap. Two seconds later she'd stormed out of the room and through the front door, letting it crash closed behind her.

As the bang of the door was still reverberating, we all gazed at each other in shock.

"Well," said Chloe finally, a small smile of triumph creeping on to her face. "That showed her!"

She was right. Kyra had overstepped the mark by several large, bounding steps, that was for sure.

But you know the weird thing? And this will sound weird – I felt kind of sorry for her...

Chapter 18

DON'T TRY THIS AT HOME

I was late back from lunchbreak, but that was the joy of having Friday afternoon off to finish our History project – I could wander into the empty art classroom we'd been assigned without worrying that I had to explain myself to a teacher.

Mind you, it didn't look like Sandie and Kyra had exactly hurried themselves either. All I had for company was a spooky stone angel statue that some of the Art classes must have been drawing. It looked like it should be smothered in ivy and mouldering away on top of a Victorian grave, not hanging about in a modern school, watching me with its blank eyes and giving me the willies.

Trying to ignore it, I started pushing back tables and chairs to clear a space on the floor: we had six big display posters to finish off, and it seemed like a good idea to get them all laid out together, so we could see what still needed to be done.

If Kyra ever turned up with them, that was. And where was Sandie?

Feeling slightly breathless after dragging and shoving furniture about, I perched myself on the nearest table, and gazed idly round the room. There were paintings and drawings displayed on every available space, as well as some weird and not-especially-wonderful collages made out of what looked like chicken wire and tissue paper. On top of the waist-high cupboards that ran around the perimeter of the room were dozens of half-made papier mâché ... well, *blobs*, and loads of wobbly pottery ... *things*. It kind of reminded me of home. All this room needed was a couple of cats padding about and a large hairy dog skidding across the lino floor and it would've been a dead ringer.

Thinking of home, my heart sank – a vision of our prickly encounter with Kyra on Wednesday night flashed into my head. Since then, I'd given up taking her to and from classes (she pretty much knew where everything was around school by now anyway), and we'd both done an excellent job of avoiding eye contact with each other. Chloe and Kellie and the others were ignoring Kyra too. Even Sandie said she was, but I don't think she was very happy doing it. Sandie's not very good at being mean to people. Even people who deserve it.

And now, I was about to spend a whole afternoon with Kyra. Was she going to mention anything? Or was she just going to pretend it never happened? I hoped so – it's what I planned to do, if I could get away with it. (I know, I know – I'm a coward. You don't have to tell me.)

God, I wished Sandie would hurry up. The idea of facing Kyra and having to make conversation with her on my own didn't exactly make me feel too fantastic.

My heart did a quick couple of star-jumps as I heard footsteps echoing along the corridor towards the classroom door.

Then I heard giggles.

Giggles?

Picture this: my best friend Sandie joking and chatting with Kyra Davies, as she helped her carry in our pile of posters.

Seeing me sitting on the table, Sandie's smile sank like a stone.

Kyra, on the other hand, was as bright and breezy as you like.

"Hi, Ally! All by yourself? Me and Sandie have just been having a *great* laugh about Mrs Fisher, haven't we, Sandie?"

"Mmm!" squeaked Sandie, looking wildly uncomfortable.

I said nothing as the two of them placed the posters on the table beside me and Kyra began unrolling them. But between you and me, I had this funny lump in my throat. I know it was stupid to feel so betrayed, but I did.

"We passed her in the corridor a minute ago and she's got herself the most *terrible* new perm, hasn't she, Sandie?"

Ah, *now* I could see what Kyra's game was: trying to make out to me that her and Sandie were such big mates and make me feel excluded.

That was her revenge for what had happened at my place on Wednesday night.

"I mean, what was it like, Sandie?" Kyra prompted her, acting all chummy.

"Uh ... bad," mumbled Sandie, her cheeks flushed pink.

"God, it was worse than *bad*," Kyra twittered, spreading all the artwork out across the table. "She looks like a sheep, doesn't— Oh, what a pain! I forgot to pick up all the sheets of paper with the captions printed on them! Hold on – I'll have to nip back to Miss Thomson's room for them..."

No sooner had Kyra darted away along the corridor, her top-knot of dark curls bobbing as she ran, when Sandie started blabbering.

"I haven't been hanging out with her, Ally; it's just that I bumped into her coming into school, and that's when she asked me to give her a hand bringing the posters and stuff along here and—"

"It's OK! It doesn't bother me!" I stopped her, even though that wasn't exactly true.

So far Kyra had sucked up to my sister and my brother, even our *animals*, and now it looked like she was doing her best to suck up to my best friend too.

Kyra was like my own personal vampire – sucking my life out from all around me...

"You know, she's all right, really," Sandie blinked her eyes beseechingly at me. "Before we saw Mrs Fisher in the corridor, Kyra was talking about what happened on Wednesday night and saying how embarrassed she was about just storming out like that..."

"Embarrassed about storming *out*?" I said, incredulously. "Shouldn't she be more embarrassed at turning up in the *first* place?"

Sandie shrugged and wrinkled her nose up.

"I know, but I feel sorry for her, Al," she carried on, peeking out of the door to check that Kyra wasn't on her way back already. "She started to tell me that she has a really hard time at home with her mum."

"Like what?" I asked.

I didn't sound too sympathetic, I know I didn't. But I was deliberately being like that; it was all

144

just because Kyra was totally confusing me. One minute she was bossy, aloof and slagging off anything and anyone in her line of vision, the next she was going gooey over my three-legged cat and turning up on my doorstep like my long-lost best buddy. Someone being two-faced, I could just about handle. Somebody having about seventeen faces I couldn't get my head around.

"I don't know *exactly* what's happening with her mum; she never finished telling me, 'cause we caught sight of Mrs Fisher," Sandie explained, making curly-wurly circles with her fingers around her head. "But she *did* say that when Chloe called her mean, it really hurt her, 'cause her mum calls her that too! Can you believe that? Her own *mum?*"

My first thought? I was shocked – how could someone's mum say things like that to their face? And then I had a second thought... Maybe Kyra was making it all up, y'know, just for attention or something.

If that was true then it had worked. Sandie had completely bought the story – great big squashy softie that she was.

"You don't honestly think—"

A tip-tap of approaching feet stopped me where I was.

"Right, that's everything!" said Kyra, slapping the stack of paper and a pair of scissors down on the table beside me. "Shall we get started?"

The rest of the afternoon wasn't exactly awash with pleasant conversation, which suited me fine. Kyra spotted a paint-splattered radio on the windowsill, and tuned it into Radio One. Apart from that, there was too much glueing and sticking and finishing off to do; so if we weren't talking about who was doing what, we didn't talk at all.

One thing I couldn't get over was that Kyra didn't once try to bring up the subject of Wednesday night with *me*, even though she'd been more than happy to with Sandie earlier on. It just made it more obvious in my mind that she was deliberately trying to get some attention from Sandie after all. That all this sob story about her mum was just made up. It had to be. Didn't it?

But I tried not to let the whole thing wind me up – we had to get this project finished this afternoon, in time to fix it up in the hall first thing on Monday, ready for the Drama department's first performance on Monday afternoon.

Just get through the next few hours as painlessly as possible, I kept reminding myself, as the hours ticked away, *and that'll be you finished with Kyra Davies…*

* * *

"There!" I said, sticking the *final* caption on the *final* poster.

I stood up straight, and surveyed our handiwork, all laid out on the floor in front of the three of us.

"Looks nice!" said Sandie brightly.

The posters definitely did look "nice". In the centre of each large sheet of artists' card was an A3 enlargement of a section of map, with bomb sites circled in red, and long, thin red lines trailing off to accompanying prints, enlarged from old photos, of what the individual streets looked like pre-war, along with a few images of what they looked like now.

I had to hand it to Kyra: she'd come up with a really good idea. Even if she was a pain-in-the-neck, conniving weirdo.

"Hmm, I'm not sure…"

"Not sure of what?" I asked, finding myself frowning at Kyra.

"It needs something else … it looks a bit boring like that."

Was she joking? Our project was done, wasn't it? It was twenty to four on Friday afternoon, i.e. twenty minutes to the official start of the week-end, and there was no way I wanted to start faffing about with these posters now.

"What do you mean, *boring*?" I quizzed her, stunned.

"I just think the maps don't stand out enough as a main image," she mused, infuriatingly. "I think maybe they need a border round them or something."

"Mmm ... maybe," Sandie half-heartedly agreed, before I got the chance to shoot her a shut-up look.

"Kyra, they're fine the way they are!" I protested, but she'd already walked over to the cabinets closest to us and started riffling through them.

"I know, but they can be *better*," she said brightly, pulling a big roll of masking tape out. "Look – if we paint lengths of this stuff black, it'll dry really quickly, and it'll be easy to cut it to the right length to frame each map. Sandie – see if there's any black paint ready to use in those containers over by the sink, otherwise we'll have to mix some up..."

"Kyra – what's the point of going to all this trouble?" I asked, fuming at the sight of Sandie meekly trotting off sink-wards. "It's not a competition. And anyway the only people who are going to be looking at it are the primary-school kids coming to see the play!"

"So?" shrugged Kyra. "I still want our project to look better than anyone else's. Oh, good, Sandie –

you got some!"

"Yeah, there's loads here," said Sandie, walking back towards us with a square plastic container of black poster-paint, left over from someone's artistic efforts that morning.

"See?" Kyra flashed her dark, almond eyes at me. "It's all ready for us – all we have to do is paint the masking tape and tidy away all our rubbish and we'll be done!"

I felt bubbles of irritation rise in my chest. She was just so pushy!

Just be patient for a little while longer, and you don't have to have anything to do with her again... I reminded myself, as my teeth ground together.

"Right! Fine! You know best!" I barked, trying to sound tough, but feeling a choke of angry tears making my voice wobble. "Here, give me the paint, Sandie – I'll do it!"

"Oh, no, you won't – since you seem to think it's such a lousy idea!" snapped Kyra, yanking the plastic container forcefully out of my hands.

Only I hadn't touched it yet.

It wasn't a particularly big container that Sandie was holding out – just about the right size to have held a family-sized chunk of raspberry ripple ice-cream in it (hey, I didn't guess that; the remnants of the label were still visible on its side) – but it sure held enough paint. Enough paint, that is, to send a mini tidal wave swooping up into the air.

It's amazing how far flying paint can fan out, it really is. I'd say try it sometime, but you'd have to be really stupid to give it a go.

Kyra – looking stunned – was left untouched, still clinging to the now empty plastic container. Me, Sandie, even the spooky statue watching over us were, however, covered in what might be described as *ebony* ripple.

Oh, and of course, our project certainly wasn't boring any more. Now, instead of trying to identify their own streets from the posters, all the visiting primary kids could have fun trying to guess what exactly the posters were supposed to *be*, under all those plate-sized splodges of black paint...

Chapter 19

ONE FOR ALL, AND ALL FOR ... UH-OH

"Ooooooh – isn't that the most beautiful thing you've ever seen?"

I squinted at the object Rowan was holding up. It was a small, fat, gold-painted cherub, stuck inside one of those domed snowstorm ornaments.

Rowan shook it hard, and instead of the usual dandruffy "snow" wafting down over him, a cascade of twinkling gold bits drizzled over his small, fat features.

"It's, er, cute," I commented, wondering what the gloopy liquid was inside those snowstorms. "But it's not exactly the most beautiful thing I've ever seen..."

No, that honour went to stuff like lightning crashing across the sky behind Ally Pally, or our garden in summer, when the wisteria goes crazy and covers the entire back wall in masses of trailing purple blossoms...

God. Who was I kidding? The most beautiful thing in the world to me was the one, the only (drum roll, please) Alfie.

Sigh.

"What are you looking at?" demanded Linn, appearing at our side.

"Um, this?"

Rowan held up the entombed cherub for Linn to inspect.

"Is that any good for Dad?" Linn asked sternly.

"Er, no," muttered Rowan.

"Well, what are you wasting time looking at it for? If it's not a possible present for Dad, then there's no point, is there?"

Linn should join the army. Sergeant major Love; at your service, *sir!*

The hippie-looking stall-holder stared at Linn, took the ornament out of Rowan's hands, and cradled it protectively to his chest.

"And what's going on?" Linn suddenly barked, scanning all around us.

"What?!" Rowan and I squeaked in unison.

"Where's Tor? Whose turn was it to hold his hand? I *told* you we have to watch out for him. I mean, this is Camden Market – I *told* you he could get lost in a second in amongst all these crowds!"

Rowan and I exchanged panicked glances. Whose turn had it been to look out for Tor? Obviously *she* couldn't remember any better than *I* could.

That's what an hour's worth of shopping amidst this rabbit warren of stalls and crush of people does for you – you end up suffering from the three Ds: Disorientation, Distraction and Death (by older sister, for failing to do your duty).

"I'm not lost!" came a small voice in our midst.

"Oh, thank goodness, Tor," said Linn, her shoulders sinking in relief. "Where did you go?"

"There!" he said indignantly, pointing to a spot all of twenty centimetres away.

Suddenly a surge of gawping shoppers shoved past, sending all four of us almost crashing into the snowstorm stall.

"OK. Enough. Let's get out of this for a while," Linn announced. "Let's go and get some food."

"Noodles!" yelped Tor excitedly.

"Noodles," Linn nodded at him, and off we all trotted (very obediently) behind her.

You know, it's funny with me and Rowan and Linn; OK, so we might niggle and nark at each other, but, boy, when the Love sisters gang up against the world, the world doesn't stand a chance.

There were only a few picnic-bench-type tables beside the takeaway food stalls, and all of them were full. Carefully selecting our victims (Rowan had raised her eyes and nodded towards the group of tourists sitting hugging their all-but-finished coffees) we moved in. Hovering right beside their table with our tinfoil trays of Thai noodles, we three girls started rabbiting away in the most obnoxiously loud, screechy voices we could. The tourists started twitching. They were on the verge of moving, to get away from our irritating banter, but not quick enough for Linn.

Bending down, she whispered something in Tor's ear.

"But I wan' it!" he yelled instantly. "I wan' it! *Whhhhhaaaaaaa*!"

"No! I told you you can't have it! Bad boy!" I scolded Tor in a pantomime voice, winking at my sisters from the corner of my eye.

"Let me have it! I wan' that *toyyyyyyyyyyyyy*! *Whhhhhhhhaaaaaaaa*!"

For a boy who didn't like to say much, he could really let it rip.

Loud enough, for sure, to send the tourists scuttling off – leaving the four of us with a roomy place to eat our lunch.

"Good work, Tor!" I grinned, holding my hand, palm-up, just as my sisters were doing.

"High-five!" whispered Tor, grinning as he slapped his small hand against all of ours, one by one.

"Hey, Ally – what's with the black paint in your hair?" asked Linn, twirling noodles round her plastic fork.

"I'm in mourning..." I mumbled, suddenly reminded of the disaster of the day before.

"What for?" Linn asked.

"My History project died."

"What, that thing with the bomb maps and everything?" Rowan exclaimed, raising her eyebrows.

She looked exactly like a movie star when she did that. The only trouble was, it was Minnie Mouse. She'd done her dark hair up in these two twisted knots on either side of her head that looked just like the slip-on ears you can buy in the Disney Store.

"Yes – the thing with the maps. That's the one," I sighed.

"It sounded like it would be really good when your friend … whatshername was talking about it. What happened?" Rowan asked, batting her big, girlie eyelashes at me.

Yep, Minnie Mouse.

"Yes it *was* a good idea. And she's not my friend. And her name's Kyra," I reeled off. "Anyway, it got vandalized yesterday."

"Who by?" gasped Rowan.

"Us," I groaned, slapping my hands over my face. "We were having an argument, and this container of paint flew over everything."

"Is this what you were supposed to be doing for

the Drama department's play?" Linn chipped in, as she worked out what I was talking about.

"I'm coming to see that! With my class!" Tor piped up.

"Are you, honey?" I smiled at him. It hadn't occurred to me that his primary school would of course be part of the audience.

"Well, Tor, you *could* have pointed out your sister's project to all your friends," Linn told him, "but now, you'll just have to point out a big empty space on the wall!"

"Ha, *ha!*" I muttered sarcastically at her, as Tor stood up and tootled off in the direction of the bins with his already empty tinfoil tray.

He's very eco-friendly, my brother.

But Linn was right – there *would* just be a big empty space looming on the wall of the school hall. There wasn't any time to do anything else. And boy, I wasn't looking forward to telling Miss Thomson that, first thing on Monday morning...

"Couldn't you save *any* of it? Was it *all* damaged?" asked Rowan, in-between sucking a noodle up into her mouth.

"It looked totally wrecked when me and Sandie left yesterday, but then we did have black paint dripping in our eyes at the time..."

"Did your clothes get covered in paint too?" Linn

156

frowned.

That would be her worst nightmare: having her neatly washed and pressed clothes *gunged*.

"Yeah – but they came out all right. Grandma soaked them as soon as I got in."

Neither of my sisters had been witness to my humiliation the afternoon before; Sandie and I had left the classroom as soon as we got over the shock of being splattered. I suppose it was a bit mean to leave Kyra to clean everything up, but all me and Sandie could think about was getting out of school and safely home before the four o'clock bell rang and we had a school full of people pointing and sniggering at us. Back at the house, only Grandma and Tor were privy to the state I was in. And by the time Rowan and Linn arrived home, I was in the shower, and more inclined to keep the whole farce to myself than merrily announce it to the world.

"Couldn't you try to do a rush job tomorrow and put something together?" Linn suggested.

She *would*. But how could you cram all that work into one day, never mind get your hands on all those materials? Not, likely, Linn...

"We'd need a miracle and a few extra pairs of hands to make that work," I replied flatly.

"Well, *I* could help, if you want. I was supposed to be seeing Nadia and Alfie tomorrow afternoon, but I can easily blow them out."

I gawped at Linn for a second; it always takes me slightly by surprise when she's nice. And she *is* nice sometimes – very nice. You just tend to forget it when you're used to her bossing you about every five seconds.

Gazing at my older sister in starry-eyed shock didn't last long – not when Rowan suddenly noticed who was missing.

"Er … where's Tor?" she interrupted.

"He's gone to chuck his rubbish away," I replied, pointing over in the direction of the big plastic dustbin.

Which is exactly where my brother wasn't.

Or anywhere else that we could see.

"Tor!" Linn yelled out in her best sergeant-major boom, alarming everyone at the surrounding tables.

This time, there was *no* small voice saying "I'm not lost!"

Chapter 20

SENDING OUT THE SEARCH PARTY

Imagine every neighbour in your street has their window open, and every single one of them has music blaring out. Walking along the pavement, you hear this weird mix of techno thumping, rock blasting, new age plinky-plonking, classical Spanish guitar-twanging and even Gregorian monks *chanting*, for God's sake.

Add to that the sensation of being in a crowd at a football match, only everyone's wearing T-shirts with band names and slogans on them instead of football shirts.

And that's what it felt like, pushing through the hordes of browsing punters in Camden Market, music pumping from ghetto blasters on every stall, it seemed, while I searched hopelessly for my little brother. I could feel my heart whirring at seventy million beats an hour; I was going into total worry overload. But how could I stop myself? I mean, how can you stop yourself imagining scary stuff, like faceless strangers just silently whisking Tor off to God knows where?

I consciously dug my not-very-long fingernails into the palm of my hands so that the pain gave me something else to think about. It didn't work: all that kept repeating through my head was how on earth me and Linn could ever hope to find Tor – presuming he hadn't (please, oh please) been spirited away – in this crush...

Then above all the din, my ears tuned in to a familiar sound.

Flippety-flap, flippety-flap...

I spun round to see Rowan's panic-stricken face, as she pushed and pattered through the sea of shoppers in her impractical red velvet mules.

"Ro!" I shouted at her, waving to get her attention before she was diverted off, down into a maze of stalls selling second-hand clothes.

"Ally!" she yelped, hurrying over to me with a speeded up *flippety-flap, flippety-flap*. "No sign of him?"

"No," I shook my head, noticing how her Minnie Mouse ears were unravelling as she ran. "But what are you doing? Linn told you to wait back at the tables in case he turned up!"

"I couldn't just hang about and do nothing!" she wailed, strands of hair flopping round her face as her knots unfurled. "I spoke to the guy at the noodle bar – I asked him to look out for Tor and get him to stay there if he came back!"

I shrugged. I guessed it made sense to have all three of us searching, but so far, at least two of us had had zero success, to my knowledge.

With that thought in my head, I looked down at my watch, and saw that twenty minutes had passed since we'd started the hunt. It was time to rush back, as agreed with Linn, to our meeting point by the noodle bar.

"Come on..." I motioned to Rowan. "Linn might be there already – and she might have found Tor..."

As if there was some enormous people-magnet lurking somewhere behind us, a wall of ambling shoppers surged towards us, blocking our way.

I'm not a pushy person, but all of a sudden, sheer fear made me develop elbows of steel, and I found myself ruthlessly barging my way into the oncoming crowds, carving a route towards the muddy courtyard that held the food stands.

A hand suddenly searched out mine, fingers clinging round it desperately. For a split-second, I thought it might be Tor, but the hand was too big to be his. I didn't even have to look round to know that my elder sister was relying on me to get us both through this. And right then, I felt a little bit braver, just knowing that poor Rowan was crumbling around the edges and depending on me.

Still pushing through determinedly, I gave Rowan's fingers a comforting squeeze, and felt her squeeze mine back.

Food stalls, noodle bar, Linn.

No Tor.

"What are we going to do?" whimpered Rowan, edging closer to hysteria. "What if someone's taken him?"

"Stop panicking; no one's taken him," said Linn authoritatively, although the slight wobble in her voice gave her away. "We'll split up and have another look round, then ... *then* we'll think about calling the police..."

At the mention of the police, Rowan lost it completely. Her bottom lip trembled with a life of its own, and fat, hot tears tumbled down her cheeks.

"It's OK, Ro; he'll be all right," I said softly, wrapping my arms round Rowan, being the big sister to my elder sister again.

"Brilliant," sighed Linn, her voice suddenly laden with irony. "What great daughters *we* are..."

"What?" I mumbled, grabbing a serviette that the guy behind the noodle bar was kindly holding out to help mop up Rowan's tears.

"Well," Linn explained, agitatedly, "the plan today was to get Dad a brilliant surprise, and what happens? The surprise turns out to be us managing to lose his only son..."

Chapter 21

LOST: ONE LITTLE BROTHER, HARDLY USED

London's big. London's *very* big. There are about eight million people living in London – and that kind of blows your head off when you know there are only about five million people in the whole of Scotland. (You've got to let me off if I'm out by a thousand or two; I always *was* better at History than Geography.)

And because it's big, one of the moans about London is that it's impersonal. That you could be being mugged by a bloke on stilts with fairy wings and a Bart Simpson mask and people would pass you by without helping, as if it happened every day.

Well, I don't think that's true. Like the guy at the noodle bar? He was on his own behind the counter, and could have carried on serving the queue of hungry customers hovering around his stall instead of helping us.

"Do you need to make a call?" he asked, after I'd taken the serviette from him – the one Rowan was currently soaking with tears and snot.

Now, he was holding out his mobile phone, trusting that a) we weren't going to do a runner with it, and b) we weren't going to call Australia, peak rate.

"Um, no – not right this second," Linn shook her head. "We're going to keep looking for—"

"Wait a minute – Grandma!" I burst out, gratefully yanking the proferred phone out of the noodle guy's hand.

"Grandma?" Linn furrowed her forehead. "What do you want to call her for? You'll just worry her – we might find Tor if we get out there looking again, and she'll never know—"

"No!" yelped Rowan. "Ally's right! Remember that Dad's always taught Tor her phone number, for emergencies?"

"He might have called her..." Linn finished the train of thought, as I hammered Grandma's number into the phone pad.

"Grandma?"

Linn couldn't help it; her Oldest Sister Instinct took over and she snatched the phone from me as soon as she heard me make contact.

"Grandma? It's Linn. No, that was Ally. Listen, have you— Oh, oh God..."

Rowan was clutching my hand again, so tightly that her purple-painted nails dug right into my skin.

I squeezed her hand back just as tightly. I could hardly breathe for panicking.

Try as we might, neither of us could make out what Linn's expression meant, as she muttered, "When? Is he...? But how... OK... OK..."

As she pressed the End Call button, the noodle guy and most of his customers were on tenterhooks alongside me and Rowan.

"You'll never guess where Tor is..." she said, looking as if she didn't know whether to laugh or cry.

Tor has his own way of working. It might not be the way that me, or Rowan or Linn would handle things, and he maybe isn't too great at explaining his reasoning (since he's not too fond of the old chit-chat, as you know), but whatever Tor decides to do, it always makes *some* kind of sense. Even if it only makes sense to Tor.

So, what had happened was, our kid brother had wandered over to the bin to chuck his rubbish away, when his well-attuned animal radar pricked up. Straight away, he spotted the pigeon – its wing trailing – huddled between two stalls, as it tried to escape the barrage of passing feet.

Without a backward glance at us, Tor went rushing over, pulling off his sweatshirt as he ran. One poorly pigeon found itself safely wrapped up in a green hooded top, and within minutes Tor was speeding out of the nearby exit with it, and straight into a parked black cab that he'd spotted dropping off passengers.

Looking in the rear-view mirror, the cabbie must have been pretty startled to find a seven year old and a pigeon as his next fare.

In fact, he was concerned enough to try to find out where Tor had come from and who he was supposed to be with. But it was no good; Tor kept repeating the same address over and over again until the cab driver decided that the safest thing to do would be to take him there.

Once at the desired destination, Tor had been very apologetic about not having any money, but the cab driver had to understand, he'd said calmly, that it *was* an emergency.

The cab driver had replied that he'd only let Tor off if he gave him a phone number of someone at home…

Smart thinking. Once Tor had reeled off Grandma's number, he'd scrambled out of the car, with his sickly charge still hugged tight to him. And once Tor had scrambled out, the cab driver was straight on his mobile, phoning Grandma.

"She was just about to leave for Harmsworth when I called," Linn explained, to me, Rowan and anyone else who cared to listen. "But I said *we'd* go and pick him up; we're much closer."

"Harmsworth?" repeated the noodle guy, as he took possession of his phone again.

"It's near the Holloway Road. It's an RSPCA clinic," Linn told him – and the hungry customers who were following the saga of our missing sibling.

"It's where they used to film that show *Animal Hospital* – with Rolf Harris," Rowan chipped in.

The noodle guy looked none the wiser.

"If you knew our little brother," I grinned at him, "it would all make perfect sense…"

Chapter 22

HOW TO BE MYSTERIOUS, BY ROWAN LOVE

Rowan added an extra dollop of beans on Tor's plate, right where he indicated.

On his breakfast plate this Sunday morning was a particularly fine piece of food art. A small log cabin (made of toast) sat under a sky full of fluffy clouds (scrambled eggs), with a couple of birds flying high (carved with care from a slice of bacon). Now, Tor was delicately manoeuvring the beans into a radiating sun.

"That's pretty," Linn smiled tolerantly at our little brother. "Now, how about eating some of it?"

She wasn't nagging, though. Her tone was more jokey than bossy. We were all glad to get Tor back in one piece, but Linn especially had smothered him in protective love since we picked him up from the RSPCA centre the day before. And she looked the the most shattered of the three of us after our little heart-stopping adventure; her normally pristine blonde-ish hair was unbrushed and just roughly tucked behind her ears.

I think it was because, being the eldest, she felt very guilty for losing Tor. Course, it wasn't her fault, but *you* try telling Linn something when she's already made up her mind about it. Dad was unbelievably cool about the whole thing and tried to get her to drop the guilt thing too, but I guessed she'd do that in her own time. And in the meantime, Tor was going to have to put up with getting hugged to death by her.

Speaking of Tor, he was fine, if a little quieter than usual. You should have seen his face when the three of us came running into the reception of the Harmsworth hospital; his eyes were like saucers at the sight of these deranged girls descending upon him. Later, he and Dad had a little man-to-boy chat about what had happened, and how while getting the pigeon fixed up was a noble and worthy thing to do, it really would have been better to let at least one of us girls in on the medical drama too.

The pigeon, meanwhile, hadn't broken its wing (much to the relief of Love Child No. 4), but had superficially damaged its feathery bits by doing something unwise like flying into an overhead cable. Its wound had been cleaned, its wing had been bandaged to its fat little body and it was now sitting blinking and looking bemused in the luxurious comfort of our garden shed. (I'd been woken up at six-thirty in the morning – after a sleep filled with nightmares involving Tor going missing in all manner of elaborate ways – by the sound of Tor's bedroom door squeaking open. It turned out he was heading downstairs and out into the garden, off to the shed to check on his pigeon patient for the hundredth time.)

"Hey, about Dad..." Rowan whispered, checking to hear that she could still make out the sound of the shower upstairs.

"Oh, not this business with his present again. I can't think about that. I'm too tired!" Linn whimpered, pushing her hardly touched breakfast away.

She was exhausted. She hadn't had a broken sleep like me – just no sleep at all, after the day's drama.

"But we've got to get him something – and quick," I pointed out. "His birthday's tomorrow!"

What a great day *that* was shaping up to be; a History project with no project, and a birthday with no present. I toyed with emptying my bank account and emigrating, but – sadly – you can't emigrate too far on £33.50.

Linn looked like we'd just asked her to climb up Mount Everest dragging a crateful of tinned beans behind her. Stress and sleep deprivation were playing havoc with her leadership skills.

"Don't worry, Linnhe – I've got an idea for Dad's present!" Rowan hissed excitedly, pulling her antique (i.e. old and holey) kimono dressing gown tighter round her as she sat down.

Linn *must* have been exhausted. She didn't even raise an irritated eyebrow at Rowan for using her whole name. Instead, she just stared wearily at her.

"Uh-huh," she said, flatly. "Hit us with it…"

"Aha! It's a secret! I'm not going to tell you!" Rowan grinned.

"OK, so we're all clubbing together to get Dad a present, but *you're* going to sort it out and keep it secret from us. Is that right?" I asked, trying to spell out to Rowan the ridiculousness of what she'd just said.

"Oh, I don't have the energy to play head games. Just do what you want, Ro, it's fine by me. Right now, I'm going back to bed for an hour," sighed Linn, scraping back her seat and getting to her feet. "And *you*—"

She pointed sternly to Tor, before reaching over and ruffling his hair.

"—stay put! OK?"

Tor nodded, his big brown eyes gazing up at her.

"So, what's your idea? What are you thinking of buying Dad?" I quizzed Rowan, as soon as we heard Linn's tired, slow footsteps trudging up the stairs.

"Who said anything about buying anything?" shrugged Rowan, trying to look mysterious.

Only it was pretty easy to work out what she was up to. If she didn't plan to *buy* him a present, it only meant one thing: she was going to *make* him something.

Uh-oh.

"What are you planning on making, then?" I asked.

Rowan looked a bit miffed that I'd managed to work out her mind-bogglingly complicated conundrum.

"I'm not telling you," she said haughtily. "But I need your help."

I was just about to explain to her that she was facing a no-tell, no-help showdown, when Tor – an eggy cloud stuck on the end of his fork – shushed us, and pointed out into the hall.

Dad was on his way down the stairs, whistling loudly to whatever had been playing on the radio in the bathroom.

"Meet me upstairs; five minutes – your room!" hissed Rowan, getting up and swanning casually out of the room with a piece of toast in her hand.

"What do you reckon, Tor – is she going to make him a bike out of balloons or something?" I whispered. "Or maybe individual zebra-striped, fake-fur covers for his spanners?"

Tor crossed his eyes, cartoon-style.

"Exactly," I nodded at him.

The one good thing about losing Tor (and finding him again – of *course*) was that it had distracted me from the hideous reality of facing Miss Thomson in the morning and explaining *what* we'd messed up and *why* we'd messed up. But then his disappearing act had created another problem in that we'd managed to come home from our shopping trip with a pigeon instead of a fantastic, unique birthday present for Dad. So, as I padded up the stairs to my room a few short minutes after Rowan, I decided that I wouldn't press her to tell me what she was up to, if she didn't want to spill. If she was so keen to solve our hassles and make something, then I should just be grateful, shut up and let her get on with it.

She was sitting cross-legged on my bed, staring up at the big map of the world on the wall above it.

"This," Rowan announced, as soon as she saw it was me, "would look really nice framed."

I shrugged and flopped down on to the bed

beside her.

"But if it was framed, I couldn't stick those coloured pins in it," I pointed out to her.

"Mmm, I suppose..." Rowan muttered, her fingers twirling the little crystal on the end of the silver chain she wore around her neck.

I stared at the pretty piece of rose quartz and felt one of those instant flashback memories fly into my head – suddenly I could picture another set of fingers playing with it, when that necklace used to belong to Mum.

Mum... Most of the time, I only try to think happy thoughts about her. (I know that sounds corny, but it's the only way I can handle it.) But just for a second, I got that ache for her: just 'cause she'd know *exactly* what to do for Dad's birthday. Actually, while Rowan stared at my map, I tried to concentrate really hard, and *will* an answer from her.

But nothing happened. All I could hear was Rowan breathing and my tummy gurgling.

"What do you want me to do?" I asked Rowan, breaking the tummy-gurgling silence. "How can I help?"

"I don't want you to do anything... I just want to have a look in that box you keep. Where is it?"

I knew straight away what she meant. Slipping

off the bed, I walked over to my old-fashioned wooden wardrobe and pulled out the wicker box I kept in the bottom of it.

"Guess I can't ask you what you're looking for?" I said, plonking it on the rug in the middle of the room.

Rowan slithered off the bed and on to the floor, ending up cross-legged again beside the box.

"Don't know myself till I see it," she smiled wryly.

She was coming over all mysterious again, and this time she was succeeding.

Downstairs in the living room is the proper, official record of our family life: a pile of photo albums, with pictures of holidays and birthdays and school plays all neatly stuck inside. But my box is a more random, unofficial record of the lives of the Loves. All the photos floating about in the box are rejects that never made it into the albums: out-of-focus shots of Grandma, taken by Tor, aged three; a selection of snaps of all of us girls, taken in different places and at different ages, but with the same black shadowy thumb effect ruining them all; stupid stuff like the time me, Linn, Rowan and Tor all crammed into the photo booth in Woolworth's and pulled the most horrible faces.

Apart from the artistically lacking photos, there're

school reports in there, and corny stuff like Tor's first baby tooth, all wrapped up in cotton wool in a tiny box. And in there somewhere too is a newspaper cutting; a local actress whose name I forget – who used to be in *EastEnders* or something – was promoting fitness in the borough, and ended up perched on a bike outside Dad's shop, with my dad standing beside her, both grinning cheesily at the camera.

As Rowan rummaged, I saw a Polaroid of myself at the bottom. Pulling it out, I stared hard and didn't know whether to laugh or cringe at the sight of me – aged ten – trying on one of Mum's long, flowery, hippie dresses. It had suited her, but it was so big on me that it was like looking at a picture of a rose bush with a head stuck on top.

"Right – this is it!" proclaimed Rowan suddenly, jumping to her feet and heading out of my room.

Rats – I hadn't even caught a *glimpse* of what she'd picked out...

Chapter 23

WHOSE FAULT IS IT ANYWAY?

There was a gentle snoring coming from the pile of laundry I hadn't sorted out yet in the corner of my room.

Well, at least *someone* was getting a good night's sleep, even if it wasn't me.

Yep, for the second night running it looked like my bed was going to be a snooze-free zone: last night, it was down to Tor's exploits; tonight it was down to sheer unadulterated dread of facing Miss Thomson first thing in the morning...

I propped myself up on my elbows to see which four- (or potentially three-) legged friend had invaded my space, but it was too dark to make out anything other than a cat-sized blob on my discarded white T-shirt.

I'd have seen more earlier; when I'd first gone to bed, the nearly full moon had been streaming a bluey light down through the small skylight directly above my bed. But now, it was gloomsville again, which kind of suited the way I was feeling.

Yeah, I know – I should have stuck my bedside light on and read a book or a magazine for a while till I felt sleepy, but I wasn't in the mood to concentrate on anything except what I do best: worrying.

It's a talent, it really is. There are starving refugees carrying all their worldly possessions and their grannies on their backs just to get to UN food camps. There are volcanoes, earthquakes, tidal waves (or tsunamis – see? I might not be sure of the exact population of London, but I *do* remember *some* Geography stuff!) that people have to live through and deal with (or run away from, very, *very* fast...). Anyhow, you get my drift; out there in the big wide world all sorts of big scary things happen to people on a depressingly regular basis, and all I can lose sleep worrying over is a stupid History project. Or a lack of one...

I'd phoned Sandie in the afternoon to have a moan about it, and immediately wished I hadn't. She didn't mean to, but she just made me stress out more.

"Miss Thomson's going to be so mad with us!" Sandie had whimpered pathetically. "She's going to kill us!"

Sandie was overreacting just a *tiny* bit. Miss Thomson wasn't the *Terminator* or anything.

"Well, I guess she isn't going to give us a hug and a kiss and say it doesn't matter!" I'd tried to joke.

"I feel like staying off sick tomorrow!" Sandie whined.

"Oh no, you don't!" I panicked. "You're not skiving off and leaving me to do this all on my own!"

What a hypocrite I am. I'd let the notion of skiving off drift through my head myself, only an hour before. I was only annoyed because Sandie saying it meant *I* couldn't do it.

"You won't be on your own – Kyra will be there!" Sandie had protested feebly.

"Wrong! *You*, me and Kyra will be there!" I'd corrected her.

What with fussing over Tor and helping Rowan select her Mystery Object from my box, I hadn't made my usual Sunday-morning rendezvous with Billy (and dogs) up at the Palace. So, after my less-than-comforting conversation with Sandie, I gave him a ring – just to see if he had any words of wisdom, any insightful thoughts that might put the whole thing in perspective for me.

Fat chance.

"Sssssssss…"

Billy took a long sharp intake of breath once I'd told him about Friday's fun events.

"What does 'sssssssss' mean?" I demanded.

"Only one thing for it," he announced.

"Go on, then – what?"

"Pretend you've got chickenpox."

"What?"

"Pretend you've got chickenpox," he repeated, as if it didn't sound stupid enough already. "It's better than an upset stomach; that only buys you a day or two at the most, and you'll *still* have to face the music. But chickenpox is great: you've got a legitimate reason to stay off all week, and the whole project thing will have blown over by the time you go back!"

"OK," I said slowly. "Problem one: how am I meant to convince my family that I've got chicken-pox? And problem two: how am I meant to convince my family that I've got chickenpox, since they know I've had chickenpox *already*?"

"People, um, can have chickenpox twice!" he said, unconvincingly. "And, hey, you're a girl; you've got make-up, haven't you?"

"*So?*"

"So, *draw* spots on!"

"Billy," I sighed. "Do me a favour: would you go and bring Precious to the phone?"

"How come?" he muttered, dumbly.

"'Cause Precious might have some useful advice

to give me – unlike you!"

And so, here I was, at three o'clock in the morning, trying to talk myself out of worrying by thinking depressing thoughts of starving refugees and earthquake-ravaged cities (not a whole heap of laughs, I can tell you), while my stomach was merrily clenching with tension.

How did I get in this state? I lay there in the dark, asking myself.

Because the project was ruined, I answered myself.

Why was the project ruined?

Because we spilt paint on it.

How did paint get spilt on it?

'Cause me and Kyra were niggling at each other.

Why were you niggling at each other?

Because she's in my face all the time.

Why is she in your face all the time?

Because she's mad.

Why…?

I gave up there. This mess wouldn't have existed if a certain someone had never turned up at our school to start with.

"Are you listening, Kyra Davies?" I said out loud to the darkness and the contentedly snoring cat. "It's all *your* fault…"

Chapter 24

WHO NEEDS THE X FILES?

It was one minute past nine.

I peered round the classroom door.

No one was there.

"It's empty," I hissed at Sandie, who was hovering behind me in the corridor, biting her nails to oblivion.

It was the eighth Wonder Of The World: our entire History class – plus Miss Thomson – had vanished into thin air. Like the passengers and crew of the *Marie Celeste*, one minute they'd been chatting normally, the next they'd hit some Bermuda Triangle weirdness and had been spirited away to a parallel universe.

"They'll be in the hall – getting everything set up for the play!" said Sandie.

Well, maybe not *quite* a parallel universe.

"Why didn't you remind me earlier?" I asked her, not really expecting to get a sensible answer.

Sandie shrugged and widened her Disney eyes at me.

See? I was right.

"Come on, then," I said, steering my reluctant feet in the direction of the hall and pretending my hands weren't really shaking. "Let's get this over with…"

Trudging along, I pictured my make-up bag sitting temptingly on the chest of drawers in my room. That dark pinky lipstick I'd got free off the front of a magazine … that fine make-up brush (off the front of another magazine) … oh, how easy it would have been to draw on those chickenpox poxy bits…

"Ally! Sandie!" beamed Miss Thomson, suddenly turning out of the hall up ahead and into our path.

I tried to fix something that I *hoped* might resemble a smile on my face, but it probably looked more like I had wind or something.

With every step closer to our teacher and our confession, the knot of dread in my stomach got tighter, and I had this incredible sensation like I was shrinking. At the rate I was going, I'd be ant-sized by the time I'd reached her. Just the right size for her to stomp on me with her heel when I told her what had happened to our project. (And it *would* be me that told Miss Thomson; Sandie would have just opened and shut her mouth like a traumatized goldfish if I'd left it to her.)

"Well done, girls!" boomed Miss Thomson as we drew level.

I was confused – did Miss Thomson *do* irony?

"I really like your posters – they work very well!"

I stared at Miss Thomson, waiting for her to bark "NOT!" and burst into maniacal laughter after what she'd just said.

But she didn't.

"Well, hurry along! Better give Kyra a hand putting them up – she's struggling away on her own at the moment!"

And with a bright smile, Miss Thomson was off, leaving us marooned, in stunned surprise.

There was only one thing that could explain it: it was me and Sandie who were in that parallel universe…

Chapter 25

AND HERE'S ONE I MADE EARLIER...

In the auditorium, there was lots of crashing and banging and shouting going on, as actors and technicians lost their rags due to last-minute-rehearsal nerves.

Out in the reception hall, the walls were awash with posters, photos and rambling captions describing life in our little patch of London half a century or so ago. Some of our History class, finished fixing up their efforts, had wandered off to nosey at the drama unfolding in the auditorium, while others were still faffing about, putting up, taking down and generally rearranging their masterpieces.

Me, I was sitting on a hard wooden bench, staring across the room at the six unstained posters of bomb sites.

"I still can't believe it," I said, shaking my head. "They don't look like they've been touched!"

"Well, the third and fourth ones were the worst; I had to bin them and start from scratch," said Kyra, who was also perched on the bench, in-between me and Sandie. "But the others only had the odd spot on them – I managed to wipe off the black paint almost completely. You can still see it faintly if you go up close, though."

"But when did you do it all? When did you have the time...?" I asked, in wonderment.

"Well, after you two left on Friday, I just carried on, till the caretaker came and kicked me out at teatime," she explained, her eyes staring straight ahead at her handiwork. "And I even managed to use the photocopier in the office before they packed up for the day – I re-did all the photos on *that* one and *that* one."

Me and Sandie both stared at the particular posters she was pointing at. "But you couldn't have done all that so quickly!" I protested.

Sandie was saying nothing, I noticed. I think she was still in shock.

"No," Kyra shook her head, her gaze still directed straight in front of her. "I came in yesterday afternoon too. The caretaker told me that the Drama lot were coming in to do a dress rehearsal, and he had to open the school up for them anyway, so he didn't mind if I was here as well."

I felt choked. I'd spent my Sunday getting gloomy and sinking into a pit of pessimism, while Kyra was actually doing something constructive.

How dumb did *I* feel?

"You ... you did a really good job, Kyra," I mumbled. "Thanks."

"Yeah!" Sandie sighed in amazement from the other end of the bench.

Kyra dropped her eyeline down to the floor, and scuffed at the faded lino with the toe of her shoe.

"Well..." she shrugged shyly. "I felt like I had to do it, really."

"No, you didn't," I contradicted her.

It was true; she didn't *have* to do it. She could have left the posters in the mess they were in and shared the blame with me and Sandie when it came to facing Miss Thomson. And, of course, being the new girl, Miss Thomson might have given her the easier time and saved the bulk of her scolding for me and Sandie.

"But I had to fix things – it was my fault!" said Kyra, finally staring me in the face with her dark almond eyes full of ... what? Embarrassment? Remorse? Guilt?

"It was my fault as much as yours!" I found myself arguing.

"And mine!" Sandie chipped in.

See – I told you Sandie was a sweetie. She wasn't the one who was arguing with Kyra, but she still tried to take a share of the blame. I hadn't even thought of that before...

"I'm just ... sorry," muttered Kyra turning away from me.

Suddenly, this close up, I realized what Kyra reminded me of: small face; almond eyes; light-brown skin; a sprinkling of darker brown freckles across her nose; big ears... She was a dead ringer for one of the deer me and Tor go and visit in the deer and donkey enclosure at the back of Alexandra Palace.

"Sorry about what?" I asked, twisting my thoughts back to the project and Kyra's starring role in saving it. "I just said, it wasn't all your fault."

(Yeah, I know – the hypocrite strikes again. That *wasn't* what I'd been saying to myself at three o'clock in the morning...)

"No, not about the project. Well, a *bit* about the project. But I mean, I'm sorry for being ... kind of pushy. For turning up at your house when all your friends were there and everything."

Urgh. What do you say when someone comes out with something as honest as that? "Yes – you *were* too pushy, and you *should* be sorry for turning up unannounced that night"? Maybe, but I couldn't be that hard-nosed. So I did a Sandie and just shrugged.

"I *know* I get too pushy sometimes, and I just can't help it…"

"Why not?" asked Sandie, scoring minus five for tact.

But I was glad she said it anyway. Might as well get straight to the point, instead of circling around it.

"It's just a thing I do, every time I come to a new school," said Kyra, her head hanging. "I arrive, and everyone's already got their little crowd of mates. No one's bothered about trying to get to know the new girl, so I just end up thinking that the only way to get noticed is to be sort of … pushy. And then I realize I've gone too far, and everyone hates me. And then I'm on my own for a while, till my dad changes jobs and we move and it starts all over again…"

A little cynical voice in the back of my head was whispering, "Don't fall for it – she could still be a nutter…" But what the hell. So I'm a big, stupid softie. So what.

"Must be tough," I said quietly.

"Mmm," Kyra murmured in agreement.

"How come your dad switches jobs so much?" asked Sandie, cutting to the quick again.

Kyra gave a wry little laugh, but still kept up her staring session at the floor.

"He doesn't particularly want to. It's more to do with my mum."

"How come?" I asked.

"Have you got three weeks?" she laughed, without sounding particularly happy. "With my mum, it's a long story…"

Tell me about it, I thought.

Mums and long stories … it looked like Kyra and I had more in common than I'd thought.

Chapter 26

EXTRA FEATHERS ON YOUR PIZZA, SIR?

"Look, Ro – across the road – isn't that your mate Von?"

"Where? Where?" said Rowan, scanning the pavements outside the restaurant window.

As soon as Rowan's attention was distracted, Linn gave me and Tor a wink across the table and promptly dived under it. Me and Tor looked at each other, and ducked down too.

"I can't see her..." we heard Rowan's voice hovering somewhere above us. "Where is she, Linnhe? Linnhe? Oi!"

Rowan joined us under the table, just as Linn was pulling the gift-wrapped present out of the carrier bag at her feet.

"Leave it alone!" Rowan snapped, grabbing the present back out of Linn's grasp.

"Aw, come on – tell us what it is before he comes back from the loo!" Linn whined, as we all straightened up in our seats again.

"No! You'll just have to wait!" Rowan chastised

"Now what?" asked Dad, sitting down in his place.

"Now," said Rowan, blushing with excitement, "you get your present!"

"Hey! A present!" Dad grinned, taking the package that Rowan was holding out to him. "You shouldn't have – you all gave me cards this morning; that would have been enough!"

"Don't get *too* excited, Dad," Linn laughed. "You haven't seen it yet…"

"Is this from all of you?" he asked, gazing around the table as he tore at the Sellotape.

"It's not from me, Martin; only from the children," said Grandma. "I haven't a clue what it is…"

"Join the club," I mumbled, grinning at Linn.

With a final impatient tug, Dad yanked the paper off, and studied the A3-sized framed picture in his hands.

"Wow!" he gasped, staring with amazement (and slightly twinkly eyes) at the vision in front of him.

The rest of us, of course, couldn't see what it was. All that was visible from our back-view was the blue feathery trim Rowan had edged the frame with.

"Lemme see!" said Tor, lunging impatiently out of his seat and standing by Dad's chair for a bird's-eye view of the present.

"What do you think?!" asked Rowan, looking as pink and shiny with excitement as the bubblegum-coloured balloon tied to the back of Tor's seat.

"Cool!" said Tor.

"Fantastic!" said Dad. "A family portrait! Perfect!"

Me, Linn and Grandma exchanged looks: unless Rowan had drugged us all and taken us round to the photographer's studio without our knowledge, we hadn't *got* a family portrait done.

"Well, come on, Martin," Grandma chastised him with a smile. "Share it with everyone!"

Beaming, Dad turned the picture round for us all to see.

Apart from the feather-boa-style trim, the main image in the frame was surrounded by a border of Rowan's trademark sequins. And the main image?

It was the strip of weeny photo-booth photos – the ones hauled from my box in the wardrobe – enlarged. There was me, Linn, Rowan and Tor in all our glory, pulling faces and giggling our heads off as we squashed together in the tiny space.

"Hey, Grandma – look!" I pointed out. "It's your idea; the family portrait!"

Grandma shot me an I-told-you-so! look, even if she seemed a bit dubious about Rowan's artistic efforts. I think it's safe to say she'd have preferred a nice soft-focus studio portrait from the place up on Crouch End Broadway.

"It's great!" laughed Dad. "It's just so natural! It's just how I see all of you!"

"Yeah, I got the idea of blowing these pics up on a photocopier from Ally's mate Kyra," Rowan explained. "You know how Chazza's mum's a solicitor? Well, she's got a colour photocopier in her office up in Muswell Hill, so Chazza got the keys off her and me and him went up and did this yesterday afternoon!"

I know it's silly, but I felt all choked up then.

For Rowan to go to all that trouble was amazing. And the picture was brilliant; with all of us laughing and fooling around ... well, you know – it was really nice, really special.

And the fact that Kyra had helped inspire Dad's present was kind of cool too.

You don't need to have a brain the size of a Nobel prize winner or anything to work out that I'd had a big change of heart about her since that morning. All that stuff about moving schools and never being able to make friends – that must have been really lonely for her; especially when you think she's an only child too. And though she didn't go into it too much, her mum sounded like *big* trouble. Apparently, that crack Kyra first made to me about her mum – the one about her being a professional drinker? Well, that's pretty much the way it is. At break this morning, after the decorating of the hall had been finished, Kyra told me and Sandie that her mum is more or less fairly normal, but when she starts to drink, everything changes. She said that her dad ends up being embarrassed by her mum so often – with her phoning or turning up at his work sloshed and shouting – that *that's* why he keeps switching jobs so much.

That's all she said, and neither me nor Sandie felt brave enough to push her for any more details. And bad as that story sounded, I get the feeling that there's more to it than that – Kyra did tell Sandie that thing about her mum calling her mean, after all. Well, maybe in time, Kyra will trust us enough to tell us.

And you never know; I might end up liking Kyra Davies almost as much as I *dis*liked her to start with – well, weirder things have happened...

"Happy Birthday, Dad!" Linn burst out, holding up her glass.

"Yeah, Happy Birthday, Dad!" I joined in, raising my glass, along with Rowan, Grandma and Tor.

Crashing our Fantas, Diet Cokes, Cokes and wine together, Dad made a quick speech.

"Thanks, you lot – and cheers to us all!"

A small voice chipped in as the glasses tinkled

again.

"And Mum!"

There was the tiniest hush for the tiniest moment: all three of us girls saw Dad exchange looks with Grandma.

"To your daughter," he smiled, raising his wine in the air.

"To Melanie," Grandma smiled back.

"To Mum!" yelped Tor, throwing his Coke so high that both his straws jiggled out of it.

"Mum!" repeated Linn, Rowan and me; Love children one, two and three swapping small, thoughtful smiles.

Our Mum? Don't panic; she's not dead. You didn't think she was, did you? No, she's fine (we think). That beach on the last postcard we got from her – it looked pretty gorgeous.

You want to know her story? Well, it's like Kyra said – have you got three weeks?

But you know something? Colin's sitting right beside me on the desk in my room just now, purring so hard he's hiccuping, and rubbing his vibrating head on my hand. So I think I'd better give up for now and pay him a bit of attention.

Stuff about my mum, about Kyra – and whether she turns out to be cool or a psycho – it'll just have to wait till another time…

* * *

Until then, I'll leave you with my Thought for the Day: always give people the benefit of the doubt. Unless, of course, they're an axe-wielding maniac asking if you happen to be Drew Barrymore.

Also by Karen McCombie

Stella Etc.

To: You
From: Stella
Subject: Stuff

Hi there!

You'd think it would be cool to live by the sea with all that sun,
sand and ice cream. But, believe me, it's not such a breeze.
I miss my best mate Frankie, my terror twin brothers drive me
nuts and my mum and dad have gone daft over the country
dump, sorry, "character cottage", that we're living in. I'm
bored, and I'm fed up with being the new girl on the block.
Still, I quite fancy finding out more about the mysterious,
deserted house in Sugar Bay. And what's with the bizarre old
lady who feeds fairycakes to seagulls. . .?
Catch up with me (and my fat, psychic cat!) in the Stella Etc.
series.
LOL

stella
XXX